the hot climate of promises and grace

THE HOT CLIMATE OF PROMISES AND GRACE

....

64 STORIES

STEVEN NIGHTINGALE

COUNTERPOINT

Library of Congress Cataloging-in-Publication Data

Names: Nightingale, Steven, author.
Title: The hot climate of promises and grace : 64 stories / Steven Nightingale.
Description: Berkeley : Counterpoint, [2016]
Identifiers: LCCN 2016020229 | ISBN 9781619027923 (hardcover)
Subjects: | BISAC: FICTION / Short Stories (single author).
Classification: LCC PS3564.I3637 A6 2016 | DDC 813/.54—dc23
LC record available at https://lccn.loc.gov/2016020229

ISBN 978-1-61902-792-3

Cover design by Gopa & Ted2, Inc.
Interior design by Domini Dragoone

COUNTERPOINT
2560 Ninth Street, Suite 318
Berkeley, CA 94710
www.counterpointpress.com

Printed in the United States of America
Distributed by Publishers Group West

10 9 8 7 6 5 4 3 2 1

For Elizabeth Dilly

—honesta, clarividente, maravillosa

. . . .

TABLE OF CONTENTS

PART I

PART II

PART III

PART IV

Quiero hacer contigo
Lo que la primavera hace con los cerezos.

I want to do with you what springtime
Does with the cherry trees.

—PABLO NERUDA

Paradise is of the Option.

—EMILY DICKINSON

I have never been in this place before. One
breathes differently, a new star near the sun
shines more blindingly than the sun.

—FRANZ KAFKA

The A'-shi-wi, or Zunis, suppose the sun, moon, and
the stars, the sky, earth, and sea, in all their phenomena and elements; and all inanimate objects, as well
as plants, animals, and men, to belong to one great
system of all-conscious and interrelated life, in which
the degrees of relationship seemed to be determined
largely, if not wholly, by the degrees of resemblance.

—FRANK H. CUSHING

PART I

I once fell in love with a woman I met while she was trying to burgle my house. I lived at the time in a ramshackle old wooden house near the top of the Berkeley Hills, not far from the university.

This is her story. It may be the world's shortest biography. I miss her still.

....

THE CAT GIVER

Once upon a time there was a cat burglar who worked assiduously to improve her technique of robbing houses and apartments. There are, for example, many ways to pick a lock, and our criminal friend invented new, more efficient, more durable tools before which even the most savage locks became pliant. She developed as well the ability to cut artfully, almost surgically, through the most ornamental window glass, so that there would be no breakage, and so that no house need suffer the offense of fragments or splinters. Often she would, after stealing what she pleased, considerately replace the cut window-pane with fresh glass she had prepared specially for the purpose. Before too long, she began to redesign whole windows, and install them furtively, so that the inhabitants of the burgled house might observe the world through a more beautiful aperture.

So delightful to her were these tricks that she began to invent more of them; and she became so entranced by the effort that she often neglected to sell in the underworld the goods she had so improperly acquired.

One time she posed as a florist and sold potted plants and trees to people whose goods interested her. Her studies in biology and horticulture had enabled her, after painstaking genetic experiments, to cultivate flowers so iridescent that tropical rainbows began to study their colors. These blooms became everywhere prized, though they had one noteworthy weakness: they perished quickly unless exposed to a flow of fresh night air. Coincidentally, the windows left open to give the splendid plants life also gave entry to a certain notorious and scholarly burglar.

Now, as she burgled, she was extremely selective. She would examine fastidiously the goods in a house and take only those which met her standards, as to integrity of design, harmony of proportion, delicacy of color, and durability of materials. Sometimes she took nothing at all. Sometimes she would leave one of her newly bred, rare plants, one that would infuse a room with a finery of color and luscious fragrance and complement the flora she found already in place.

Another ruse of hers was to design and manufacture her own locks—superb ones that made a house well-nigh impenetrable. Impenetrable to everyone, of course, except the lock designer. Now these locks were so ingenious and intransigent that advanced versions came to be used on safes, on big vaults at important banks, on the security doors at the great compounds where national treasuries were kept. In fact, so respected were these instruments that our cat burglar was summoned urgently hither and yon, to distant lands and curious nations, to sell and install her locks. So busy was she making the world safe from assaults upon treasures public and private, that she hardly had time to threaten us with her fine and enthusiastic criminality.

All of this was just as well, for her stock of stolen goods had, over all this time, grown immensely; and she next determined she would use her felonious and impeccable talents to distribute them where they did the most good. So did she become a cat giver: people who had once lost things to her would find in their house other goods, chosen to be more useful to the cause of strange living. And other people, strange already but lacking in some truly necessary item, would come home to find a new chair in their apartment, a cooking stove, a basket of food, a computer, a shelf of carefully chosen books, an uncanny watercolor on the wall; or even a medicine to take, so as to arrest an illness they did not yet know they had.

There were other duties: sometimes, when a bank was defrauded and threatened with default, our burglar would go to their vaults and replenish their funds. Occasionally, also, the problems with the international balance of payments were so intractable and wearisome that she was obliged to travel wildly around to redistribute money among countries.

One day the forces of law and order caught our cat giver in a house not her own, installing a safety latch. She was doing so because, without this certain door latch, the little girl who lived there would, the next day, have wandered outside and drowned in a nearby ditch. The authorities did not, of course, believe her story; and she was tried, convicted, and sent to prison. On the way to her cell she stole the guard's keys; and so was able, over the years, to visit all her fellow prisoners at the facility and teach them her arts. The prison became notorious as the breeding ground of most of the cat givers now at large in society.

And so our dear world, that once so feared crime, now must confront an even more desperate and perilous situation: that in spite of all its efforts, it will not be able to prevent good from being done.

I had asked a woman in Seattle (she worked in the Elliott Bay bookstore) why it had come to be that I was living in what felt to be a crossfire of stories. She laughed at me, and then told me this story. Then she looked at me and wished me the best, and then laughed again, I suppose at having to deal with such a simple beast.

....

STORY OF THE STORY

Once there was a story that never got told, and because of this she was lonely and sad. The only thing she could think to do was to go out and ask someone to tell her, even just once, in hopes that she might be remembered, and told later by someone else. So our story put on some old clothes and set off down the road.

The first house she came to, she walked right up to the front door and knocked. Now, in this particular house there lived people who were suspicious of strangers—especially those who had no certified occupation. So when they called through the door to ask what she wanted, and when she began shyly to answer—well, I am a story and I'm confused about the future and was wondering if maybe you could help me figure out how it is that I might be told, and ... The occupants of the house opened the door and drove her away with cudgels.

And so she went to the countryside, where it was safer for stories, and there decided to go to a farm and ask for work, so as to get to know the people there before she revealed her true identity and asked them to tell her. And sure enough, the farm family gave her work—milking cows, shoeing horses, eating apples off the tree, pruning orchards, drinking hard liquor, and raising hell in town. All this was so much fun that our story never did get around to telling her employers that she was not a person at all, and only wanted to be told by someone, and to give people joy. And when time came to move on, she found herself much altered; that is, the story she was had changed.

Our friend went to many houses, worked many jobs, and generally tramped around and had a fine time. She even told a few stories herself, so that she could gain a sense of what made some stories worth telling. Doing all this, she changed a lot, and wanted more desperately than ever to be told, for she was getting to be such a long, complicated story she could hardly keep track of herself.

In fact, as she made herself a life, as she gathered into herself from the events of every day the common-place, powerful workings of the world, the story that she was came to be in ferment, remaking itself continually, gaining new contour and detail, taking on a vitality of its own—until she saw that only by the life that she lived could the story that she was be told.

So it was she learned that stories turn into the world. It was not true that stories are part of the world; rather, the world is composed of just those stories we are, the ones we use and honor and learn. That is, the world is composed of what these stories mean; and we, the story people, as we live, are saying how we think everything is arranged—what might happen, the way hope might be recovered, whether our promises count, how heaven is hidden or comes forth; whether we can understand our origin, amusement, sorrow, and deliverance.

Thus is the life we choose more disconcerting and extraordinary than many would wish: for it turns out that, whatever we do, day by day and in every minute too, by our every thought and every action, whether we want to or not, we are telling each other the truth.

A story told to me in a brusque way by a classical scholar,
an Englishwoman living in the town of Cortona, near
the border of Tuscany and Umbria. The town has in its
small museum a spectacular, golden Annunciation by
Fra Angelico. I wondered if the painting gave some of its
spiritual luminosity to the story.

 My learned friend related the whole tale with great
surety and rapidity, as if it held the most obvious expla-
nation in the world.

....

WHY CERTAIN WOMEN
SPURN MIRRORS

Once there lived a people whose knowledge of the world surpassed anything we know of today. They had come to this knowledge by their ability to change the most basic ideas about themselves. They changed them even to the point of altering their bodily form, which transformation was possible because, as everyone knows, we are composed of gifts, capacities, possibilities, energies, all arranged in a temporary form called *flesh*.

 By such changes, our citizens could turn into anything in the world, anything in all this world. They might be able to exist for a spell of time as different plants, different animals; as different kinds of weather (like a cyclone or soft rain); even as different people, so that the breadth and astonishment of their experience could take on the framework of different hearts.

In this way there was a free exchange of life between all the participants in life; a concerted movement of unity and devotion—the very movement, we might say, of learning.

One day, however, amid these fabulous improvisations, one of these people invented the mirror. The function of mirrors, of course, was to show everyone just as they appear—that is, as they have created themselves—at that precise moment. Unfortunately, many people were persuaded by this marvelous invention that they really did always look like that. Because of this horrific and obsessive error, with its selfish disobedience to light, the radiant circulation of learning became less and less visible and conscious. And eventually, for most of us, the continual transformation stopped, and the natural unity of creation seemed to split into many sovereign lives. In fact, today, in our times, few of the original race survive.

These few still contrive to rid the world of mirrors. It is very odd, they say, that so many think when they look into a mirror that they see themselves, rather than merely one of the experiments of light, a luminous gift, a guess, a proposition, a work-in-progress. It is as if each person (though it is shocking to have to write such a thing)—each person felt that his image was in fact himself, that the possibilities of life ended at the boundaries of that picture, that all her vision and understanding and love had their source in that one form, her very own.

It is as if when people walked, they never felt the earth, just their feet; as if when they looked, they did not see the world, just their eyes; as if when they loved, they could love no one but themselves.

Sierra Valley, California, is a paradise for birds, and in general reminiscent of heaven. An extraordinary woman there has designed and built her own house with wood from trees she selected, cut, and trimmed herself. She told me this story when I asked her why she thought that working in construction was so important.

....

WHAT THE WOMEN BUILT

Once there was a woman who, with certain of her compatriots, had her own construction company. In the houses they built, there were always more stairs than were necessary. In a one-story house, the inhabitants would find a stairway leading to the second floor, which did not exist. In a larger, two-story house, stairs would be built at the back of closets, or at the side of the attic. All the extra stairs seemed to go nowhere. This confused many people. But these inconceivable steps were seldom spoken of, since all of us would rather talk about what we presume we understand.

The stairs were artfully constructed, with a curious patterning of inlay, suggestive curves and angles, uncanny proportions. It was hard to know what to do with them. They were thought to be some recondite structural component of the house, or an idiosyncratic touch of an anonymous craftsman, or the decorative adventure of an unknown architect. Of course, people in such a house would get accustomed to using only those ways of ascent useful in their lives, and so the unused ones were relegated to the twilight of improbability and neglect; until it was just as if they didn't exist.

Every now and then someone in a rare state of mind, someone whose understanding had begun to respond to daily, homely fact, would come to notice these extra stairs. After the required study and preparation, one day that person would ascend them. If anyone saw her go, no special attention was excited, because it is hard to think there is any danger in climbing stairs that do not exist.

By such climbs something was created: at the top of the stairs, in the wall or ceiling, a door would appear; and through it our climbers would go. They found, as they had hoped privately and for so long, that these secret stairs led to a room in another house. In fact, all the secret stairs in the world led to one or another room in this special house. This being so, during their visit our climbers met people from distant lands, who, by a natural development of commonsense skills of living, had done the central, necessary thing—they had rid themselves of themselves. In doing so, they had thrown off the melancholy and bitterness that in our day pass for marks of a serious mind. So were they able to have new lives of impeccable kindness, easygoing clairvoyance, and powerful account. Some of these people, it is said, were librarians who could read your mind when they shook your hand, and then would know how, mischievously, to be most helpful to you. Some traveled along with the wind because there are ideas we can earn only if we are invisible and far-rambling. Some of them, called upon to live for a spell of time in deep space, had learned how to garden among the stars. Others who worked as marine biologists might carry all the oceans in the pockets of an old coat.

In this house, all these people shared just such common capacities and taught one another a way of gift-giving that was bound up with blessings and adventure.

Now from the many doors of this meeting-house (which was nowhere, since it could only be entered by means of stairways that led nowhere) a person could leave and find herself in many different parts of the world, following almost any occupation. And some would do so, and in that way of traveling take up new lives of secret purposes. The rest would return down the old stairs to their old houses and resume a life that was apparently the same, but was never the same.

As for the original builders, they prospered greatly and secretly, and all of them are now retired. Some of the climbers of the special stairways have taken up the work the builders are now too old to do. There are now, for example, in many cities, streets you will not find on any map, which lead to other interesting and habitable planets; and factories that do not seem to produce a visible product, because they produce winks, tricks, dances, and metaphors. We should mention, as well, a house on a superbly hidden street, where a woman is writing a sacred text that will be used to correct and update, at long last, all the sacred texts we presently have.

And there have been some special projects: in the sealed basement of an old house it once became necessary to construct a chain of tropical islands set in a luminous and merciful sea. One descendant of the original builder, it is said, has even constructed an entire university between two petals of a flower.

Of course, many people, especially the men who own rival construction firms, claim that such things do not exist because, just like the magical stairs, they are not useful to everyone. The female contractors, though, just carry on with their indispensable, hidden work. And they express certain doubts about the virtues of self-evident usefulness.

For example, the hearts of men, are they useful? And if they are not useful, do they exist? And if they do exist, where are they all?

*The Book of Genesis, of course, exists in many versions;
and creation stories in the Near East, and world-
wide, have now been much studied. In New Orleans I
attended some talks at a gathering of theologians, who
seem to have, as a group, an abiding affection for gumbo
and rum drinks.*

*I asked a scholar of the Bible what understanding
she had developed of the actions of Eve; and she told
me this story.*

....

EVE: WHY WE LOVE HER SO MUCH

She was mostly alone in the world, which was not a bad
thing, because of the intricate and tranquil detonation of
beauty everywhere around her. She studied the flora in all
the minutiae of its divinity—she loved the garden. And in
order to show that love, she asked the help of the animals.

She asked Adam, but he was not always curious.
He was, in fact, rather satisfied with himself and his
own conceptions, and sometimes had no particular
inclination to engage with the garden; or, in fact, to
explore what kind of outlandish collaborations of mind
he might have with his companion. Eve, as someone
who could conceive and bring forth life, knew what

he could never know—she knew that risking your life is necessary and obvious. She knew that they should study their home grounds, that beauty is conceived and sustained by adventures in love, that perfection of place is a natural complement and outcome of the completion of soul.

She knew that if they learned, urgently and everywhere, all they could in the garden, then whatever their fate, they would have a better chance.

So when the snake, who knew life when she saw it, and would have helped Eve in anything, told her the location of the Tree of the Knowledge of Good and Evil, she ate of its fruit and became wise. She even gave some to Adam, who, in his desultory way, ate some: and so they were wise together.

And what then did they do, this wise woman and man? They made aprons of fig leaves. And why? Contrary to what we have heard, it was not because they were ashamed—a ridiculous, unsupported idea. It was partly because they wanted to make something for one another; but it was mostly because each of them, having tasted of the fruit, saw that the other was beautiful. They wanted to cover this beauty, so as to make its uncovering more various, more teasing, more storied; because, being wise, they saw how the good world may be kept alive in the playfulness of a couple in love.

Into this happy scene came God, trudging along, in a bad mood. He called for them, and Adam, who still could get nervous, and like men everywhere wanted to please the boss, went ahead and spilled the whole story. Whereupon God, seized by the most unfortunate temper tantrum in history, started hollering.

After He had finished with a whole set piece of excited pyrotechnics and rousing calumny, He came to His senses and recognized that He should get down to business, because He had real problems: if this thoughtful and adventurous pair, already wise, and delighted with one another, ate now of the Tree of Life, they would be *as gods*! Yikes! What were they thinking? Didn't they understand that only He could be the one cockerel, the one swashbuckler, the one cloud-draped protagonist in this story? Worst of all, what if they discovered the truth about Him? That His Name referred to a knowledge that, by means of their work and love, could belong to them? That it was their origin and destiny? *As gods! Then* what would He do?

So, wanting to protect His recently conjured theological monopoly, He hustled them from the garden with appropriate curses and arranged for the fragrant and lovely floral center of creation to be protected by angels and flaming swords. Adam and Eve, left alone at last, went straight to bed; and the rest is history.

But some have pointed out that Eden was not forbidden to anyone else, and that the beauties of Eden were protected forever. Others have noted that although the Tree of the Knowledge of Good and Evil was forbidden to Adam and Eve, the Tree of Life was never forbidden. And some say that before eating of the forbidden fruit, one of our couple had already eaten of the Tree of Life.

Which is why women have that smile.

One of the stories told by a woman about herself. She was irresistibly intelligent, sexually effervescent, and for years afterward, on sunny afternoons, when I closed my eyes, even briefly, I would see her. She lives in the Dutch Antilles. I have simply never known anyone with such an easygoing, offbeat genius for life.

....

THE WINDSWEPT
MORNING OF JULIANA

Juliana, who lived on a tropical island near the beach, was not contaminated by the pessimism that turns up everywhere, like a dash of arsenic in all our food. She never had known the rank poison of despair. Rather, her days rolled along with the standard joys and certainties, stopped only by moments of amused clairvoyance: sometimes, grains of beach sand looked to her recognizably like planets full of the most bounteous life.

Her boyfriend, she had sent away, for being too goal-directed. But at least he had sought the midmost of her pleasures, and wanted to dwell at length in those blessed regions; so that she remembered with thankfulness how, after his devotions in the moist nights, she had lain loose and shining in the moonlight.

In the morning, every morning, she swam in the ocean. She loved the cool green water, the sting of the salt, the sense of envelopment and welcome and relief.

In other words, an ordinary woman.

And so it was, in her ordinary way, Juliana woke up one morning and thought: Wait a minute! This business about heaven, what if it's all a trick, to tempt us to look far away? What if the next world was here, right under our noses? What if it's in the kitchen, on the front porch, or comes by with the birds? And she leapt out of bed and went to see.

As she was doing so, she heard a knock on the door. It was a man claiming to have answers to her questions.

"And who the hell are you?" she asked in her circumspect way as she threw open the door.

"I am a cyclone," he answered amiably. And, barging right in and turning before her eyes into a miniature version of the huge coiled storms that passed over her island, the man rotated through the house, swishing the bedclothes, blowing her skirts all over the place, knocking over cups, and nearly stripping from her the light robe she was wearing, beneath which she was naked as the sun and moon. All this he did with a roaring that, she noted, had a kind of surly playfulness.

Metamorphosed again into a man, he stood before her.

"Now you know," he said.

"What do I know?" she asked, hanging onto her robe.

"You've cracked the riddle," he said.

"Have we been properly introduced?" she asked.

"You've gotten the joke!" he added triumphantly.

"Is this whole show some kind of offbeat amorous overture?" she wondered aloud.

"Yes indeed," he said, "the whole show." And he kissed her full on the mouth, a kiss of salt, wind, and moving skies. A girl could not help but be a little intrigued.

She meditated on her next move. She looked at the cyclone before her. He grinned.

"Oh for heaven's sake," she said, and she threw off her robe and took him straight to bed, where as she had guessed he proved to have a sustained and cyclonic style.

Pleasure, Juliana thought, was meant to be just this rough, spiritous movement, the turning and building, the fine, enfolding, irresistible light, the upwelling power with a peace at its center.

As they lay in bed later that morning, she asked him: "What riddle?"

"The trick, the joke; the simple thing, the hope," he answered, and she noted acerbically to herself how, after love, all men get vague.

"It appears," she said intemperately, "that the distinctions we have heretofore taken for granted, such as those between heaven and earth, nature and culture, man and woman, love and knowledge, are no more than mere habit, sloth, assumption, and plain stupefaction; and have no logical necessity, nor ontological legitimacy. This being so," she concluded, "everything is changed."

And he grinned at her once more, and so their conversation went, until she slipped over on top of him and over his face let loose a stream of kisses—long ones, of real suavity and spiciness.

And that is why it is said everywhere: any knock at the door means the world is looking for you.

And that is why it is said everywhere: if you are ready, everything is ready.

And that is why it is said everywhere: religion begins at home.

*A translation of the shortest story told to me by a
Maroon—a healer who is a descendant of escaped
slaves—in the tropical forest of the Blue Mountains
in Jamaica. The range is full of fireflies. Some nights it
seemed as if the whole forest was weightless with their
luminous weaving.*

*Like most of her compatriots, the Maroon was a stu-
dent of the traveling light around her.*

*I cherish this story because, so long ago, it marked the
beginning of all these stories.*

....

WHERE ARE YOU GOING?

The earth receives a windfall of light, an extravagant,
storytelling fortune of light, every day; but little of it
falls upon any one man.

Every day, the people of this earth attend with great
skill, study, and deliberation to what they presume to be
their personal and important affairs.

They presume so out of a belief that because they
can see and appreciate what they are themselves doing,
they do not need to learn where the light is going.

In the narrow canyons of northern California, the Feather River falls from the Sierra with otherworldly exuberance. The woman who told me this story was a river guide, and so she knew the water's work and ideas.

....

WHAT SHE MEANT

Our friend Emily was known as an eccentric, so we think it important you hear her story. Her eccentricity goes back to a time when as a young woman she walked every day at dusk along a river near her home, almost as if she were by her dedication trying to be the accomplice of the clear currents. She would take her walks to meditate upon the events of the day, which, like all the human world, she found usually to be a mixture of tomfoolery, useless complication, and impressive savagery. That is to say, she viewed things as do all young people, and people not so young, who have not been pinioned by the practical world—she walked along and wondered how she would ever be truly useful.

As she walked, she would talk incessantly to herself, and those who happened by her would think that her insanity was so well-controlled and inoffensive that it could almost be called quaint. And when, after three years, she went quiet, the people accustomed to her talking thought that maturity had finally applied the usual correction to the errant young woman. But, to tell the truth, Emily was beset by another destiny entirely: a new voice had come to her, a new voice inaudible to most of the others walking by the river—which was comical, since it was the voice of the river itself.

"Emily," said the river, "I thank you for stopping your monolog."

"Then you *were* listening," said Emily, in tears of relief that her secret hope had not been held so close, for so long, in vain.

"I thought I would never get a word in," said the river.

"I wanted to make sure you would hear me," said Emily.

"Come with me now," said the river.

And it was then, moving to a rhythm drawn from the accumulated music of her walking, using finally the energy that she had learned from the shining that marked everywhere the waters—it was then she walked to the river's edge, paused, put one foot into the currents, and felt, step by step, as she walked, the founding of a path; as she turned, step by step, into water.

She had always hoped a woman could learn from a river; she needed to know what a river knows. The long travels of snowflakes and raindrops moved through her understanding, and she was taught, as she tossed her way along, the histories of all the rocks, and their futures. She was the straight stream and the reluctant eddy, learning to pirouette before the rising bank and uncoil midway into the mainstream; to stretch out with power in the narrows and then quiet into wide, clear currents; to bear all the images of city and countryside, so as to mix them into her moving story. She learned the perfect hymns brought by passing waters; she saw the way the river, by masterful whimsy of running on, directs an ancient puppetry of driftwood. And she herself ran on, doing the ordinary work of rivers: fanning into a screen that might bear miniature rainbows, and polishing pebbles on the riverbed.

Best of all were the rapids: to break up and be always the same; to burst on high and lose her way, knowing she could find it again down in the decisive currents.

And so, chaotic and lawful, broken and healed, at peace and aglide, she stepped out of the river and walked home.

Everyone thought Emily eccentric. We thought she was too, because we didn't know her story until much later, and then a lot of things made sense. We remembered her saying to us: my friends, my friends, I will love you as long as the river runs; and it's nice, now, to know what she meant.

Some years ago I took a bus from Boston to New York City. For a time I sat next to a woman, recently widowed, who gave me this brief account in a slow, reflective way, the way honey spills from a jar. That is, she spoke with a rare combination of regret and joy.

....

HOUSEHOLD AFFAIRS

Some people save all their odds and ends by putting them in a big closet. Then, when the seeker opens the door, he may with luck and patience find in the irregular, teetering galaxy of things there, some long-lost and desperately sought-after item.

One man, against the advice of his wife, stored all the truths he discovered in a big closet. When he opened the door one day, he was destroyed by a boiling-forth of terrible fires.

That is why it is said everywhere: while things can be saved, the truth must be used.

This woman told me this story long after I had met her. It explained many curious things about her, especially her uncanny clarity, her daily search for beauty, and her feral seriousness. She told me this story in Dublin, in Ireland—a country that has had its share of apocalypse.

....

MAN, WOMAN, DOG: A LOVE STORY

Because of my boyfriend's pet, my house was destroyed in a terrible explosion, and I have killed someone. We had moved in together, and he had brought his dog. I had misgivings about our love affair, but I could not trace them to any source. Now, of course, I know better.

The dog, whom he had named Constantine, was a raucous little mutt, muscular and confident. One day we discovered a small bleeding rash on Constantine's back. It was odd, the blood, because the rash was in a position where the dog could not reach it with his claws or teeth, so there was no obvious explanation for its being so raw. The rash was small.

I wanted to take the dog to be treated, but my boyfriend refused.

We did not notice at first how the rash grew, since, as it grew, so did the dog. And so did the quantity of blood. And we took no account of the disappearance of the dog of one of our neighbors. Nothing was left of him but a bloody spinal cord.

One day, seeing Constantine's shadow, I thought he had at least doubled in size. Checking the rash, I found that it had changed in texture: ragged scales, sharp and repellent, had extended themselves beneath his fur. And that was not all. Constantine's snout was now elongated, and there were two long swellings on his back. And something else that I could not explain. I mean my fear.

I explained all this to my boyfriend. I asked him to leave, and to take Constantine with him. To demonstrate that nothing was wrong, he called his dog, who came obediently to him, and they sat together on the couch and nuzzled each other. It was a picture of animate bliss. They even kissed each other.

Many people can recount how time slows during a horrible accident. The car that crushed their legs seemed to approach with infinite slowness; the punch that put out an eye came round as though dreaming of damage; the knife that severed a hand descended in an arc with the grace of ritual dance. So it was over the next weeks.

The four-year-old boy who lived next door was cooked before he was eaten. To be more accurate, he was blackened in a burst of fire.

It happened the same day when I got home to find, in our living room, a demon of classical power with a remarkable resemblance to the nightmares of just such children. A moist snout, scales pulsing and filthy, two ferocious wings held above his heaving body, lava in his mouth. By the side of this marauding carnivore, gazing at him with the adoration of a lover, stood my boyfriend. He was naked to the waist, so that I could see his lovely, muscular form. I could also see the bleeding rash on his chest. He seemed to have grown taller.

I had not watched all this fun without preparing everything. I had, in fact, filled the basement of my house with explosives. The detonator was out in the backyard, near the peach tree. I turned and walked out. They both looked longingly at me.

The grotesque, blooming explosion that killed them was so hot, almost nothing was left of them.

But my love is left. I was meant to love them in just the way I did. What would they have done without me? What would you have done?

Do you understand? We are in danger, right now, of losing everything. All the cut-loose beauties, every wild chance at cherishing, the music in morning light, the passage of heavens through our flesh, the working of minds in concord with one another, the goodness at midmost of the world, our birthright, homeland, hearts; our hope.

Everything. Do you understand?

*At an exhibition of pre-Columbian art in Santa Fe,
New Mexico, I fell into conversation with a woman who
told me of the discovery of the ancient Nag Hammadi
texts in the sands of Egypt, where one can see the beginning of a change in our idea of the life of Jesus, and of the
movement of learning in the mind. These extraordinary
texts, pre-doctrinal and indispensable, have among them
important writings by women. She directed me especially
to one called "Thunder: Perfect Mind," a piece of riddling,
transcendent poetry.*

*I asked her to tell me about the most extraordinary
person she had ever met; but I was hardly prepared for
the account here that was her answer.*

....

THUNDER: PERFECT MIND

To watch a lighting storm over wild country is to be
inspirited by cut loose beauty and irresistible good times.
It is as though the earth and the sky take upon themselves the task to form the lines of light that bring them
together urgently and irresistibly. Often we wonder what
happens at the site of so many hot electric strikes. Who
knows? But for one strike, in the deserts of New Mexico,
on the sandstone rimrock of a canyon, I know what happened. The storm cleared, and where the bolt had struck,
there stood a woman.

You may be skeptical about this; but it is no more unlikely than, say, brain surgery.

I was camped well away from the canyon where the woman stood, but I thought it hospitable to go and welcome her to the wilderness I knew so well and loved so much. As I approached her, I could see that she was plain, and as I neared her she said:

"Could you take me into town for some toast and honey? And maybe later a warm whiskey?"

Now, I was not about to deny a woman born out of a lightning bolt. I led her to my pickup truck, we rode into town to a little café, and she sat quietly, watching everyone. All this while, we did not talk; although I could not take my eyes from her. I had never seen such fantastical tranquility.

Finally I had to ask:

"What are you doing here?"

"I need to deliver some paint," she replied immediately.

"Paint?" I said skeptically. I told her it sounded a bit pedestrian. I got a rambunctious laugh from her.

And then she said, as if it were an explanation:

"Every now and then, because it is necessary, a woman—even, now and then, a man—changes herself so essentially that the lucent, humble, learned part of us comes to saturate all the tissues of the body. Someone changed in this way shines, though the light is not visible to everyone. But to those who can see, she shines like a—well, it's obvious."

"Yes?"

"—like a lightning bolt."

"And how are you going to find her?"

"How do you become aware of the presence of lightning, when you cannot see it?"

"You mean . . ."

"I mean we listen. When she comes suddenly into her place of work, then if she is a bolt of pure light, you will recognize her by the rolling of thunder through the room."

I TRAVELED AROUND with my newfound friend—let's call her Bolt. We listened to talk in bars, to local gossip, to tall tales. Finally we heard a rumor about a delightful and amusing show for children.

So it was that we found her, in a little town far out in the backcountry of the American West. She was an elementary school teacher. When she walked into class in the morning, an almost florescent thunder careened through the schoolroom, making the children cry out in joy and wonderment.

Everyone, of course, thought that the teacher had a recording hidden somewhere; and so no one inquired further. Thus was her protection assured.

We waited until the last child had left the classroom to go home. The teacher was correcting some papers when we walked into the room. Bolt waved her arm and thunder rocked the schoolroom, spilling books from the shelves.

The teacher—call her Ella—came forward immediately to meet us. She scrutinized Bolt. I watched them both, as they shimmered together. I knew I could see only a part of their radiance.

"I've found you!" exclaimed Bolt mischievously. And she took from her overalls a small can of paint.

Ella looked at the can carefully, turning it over in her hands, gently, as though she hardly touched it.

"Can we try it?" she said immediately.

"We must!" replied Bolt.

They walked over to the mirror in the room, which was placed opposite another. Ella had a habit of showing the children the variety of infinite reflections they could set up when they stood between the mirrors. Their images reproduced and went off into the depths of the silver surfaces like laughter into a pool.

Now Ella went over to one of the mirrors and, using a child's brush, daubed a thin coating of the paint upon it. Then she did the same with the other.

The two women stood in the middle between the two mirrors. I went to look, and I was nearly blinded by the image of them, two torches of light that passed into the clouds, ragged garlands of light that hung from heaven to earth, riptides of light that surged from the floor into the sky.

I could see myself, a little gleam. I was ashamed. Ella came over to me immediately. I wanted to hide.

"The paint allows the mirrors to show the full picture of a person, rather than the poor sketch we are accustomed to see. What you see there is what I can see all the time, when I look at other people."

"Why do you need it then?" I asked, a bit intemperately.

"So that she can show other people to themselves," answered Bolt.

"And why do that?" I shot back, out of my shame.

"So that they might find the kindling within them and begin their learning of the responsible luminosity and power that binds together earth and heaven," answered Ella gently.

So it was that I became Ella's student, as if I were a child. Ella, with her paint, was able to persuade some others to join our clandestine and unusual class, which she held in the elementary school just after the children had gone home.

Bolt comes to see us. I must say, sometimes the classroom is a bit thunderous. Rather like a playground. Their teaching has such a bright current of playfulness that if you were not fully prepared, it would kill you.

All I can tell you is that there is a sensibility in light, a raucous surety in such teaching, a way to burnish the body back to its once and future state.

All I can tell you is to pay more attention to the weather report.

This story was offered to me by a woman who was convinced that there exists another domain of law, unwritten but potent, of which our common law is a crude but useful expression. This, I think, is a variant of the Sufi idea that underlying our five senses are five more potent capacities of mind that allow us to integrate our minds, and know a homecoming of soul.

This woman held that these laws could be learned, and that, in any case, we are governed by them. She practices law in Philadelphia. She is a plain, able woman; that is, irresistible. I had asked her how her twin sister met the artist she married.

. . . .

IN ORDER TO
OBEY THE LAW

Once there was a painter who wanted to see things as they really are. He wanted to set himself aside, to paint everything for itself, in the most lucid and comprehensive detail. The problem, he decided, with wanting to see anything finally, truly, clearly, is that when we try to do so, we have to stand someplace, at some time. And, standing there, we see what is around and behind the object of our contemplation, we see it from a certain angle, at a certain moment of the day, in a certain light, in relation to whatever else is going on at the time. So do our perceptions become selective, reduced, personal.

His method, by contrast, was to give to his watching the richest possible variety, to watch at all hours and in all circumstances, so as to gather the widest, most numerous, most contemplative views of one thing; and then to unify those views as he painted. By such means, he hoped, the things of the world might come forth with their own substance, reality, and harmony.

He once painted a peach tree; and painted himself, unbeknownst to him, right into this little story.

He first found the peach tree in early spring seen against snowy mountains. He noted then the coruscations of rain along the branches, the adolescent suppleness of its form, the lovely buds. In the next several weeks he walked slowly around and around the tree, and stayed close to see how the color of the blossoms changed with the angle of the light. Then in midsummer, just as the fruit was getting heavy, he visited the tree again, sketching the way the branches bowed slowly with the weight of the fruit. When the peaches were ripe, he was ready to commence his painting. And, weeks later, just as he was finishing work in the warm green meadow, he saw the woman, walking easily, come close to the tree, touching a peach with her fingertips. He saw the way her hair and the leaves glistened together. And in the midmost of that late summer day, in front of him, she picked and ate a peach, the juice of the fruit shining on her mouth. She looked at him with independence, understanding, hopefulness, surety.

Our painter was brought to consider a new question: what is the best way to taste peach juice?

He is meant to love her. He has always been meant to love her. But he had given up hope of having such joys on this earth, because he had not understood what she already knew. She knew that every springtime the light looks upon each of us, to see if, at last, free of the bitterness and cynicism in ourselves and of our times, we can be trusted.

Later, she was able to teach him: if you omit yourself, and by the way you work bring all the spectrum of what you see together into beauty, the world will bring a beauty together with you.

It's the law.

A selection, a rather modest selection, from two hours'
conversation with a woman who seems to talk, every other
minute, in proverbs. I was in her kitchen, in the uncanny
city of Fez, in Morocco, and she talked as she cooked an
exotic meal, including a dish with pomegranate sauce.
Of course, I had known that she conceived of cooking as
a metaphysical enterprise; hence her love of proverbs,
their words like so many ingredients to be combined in
our understanding.

....

FROM ONE DAY'S CHAT
WITH A BELOVED WOMAN

The soft peach holds a hard stone.

We walk before we run, but refuse to think that running
is a prelude to movement along the song-lines of sunlight.

Centuries have been wasted trying to set fire to the light
of our fire.

A heart within your heart will seek your amnesty.

Honey in the cupboard still is sweet.

That man, you think, is gazing prayerfully at the magnificent old oak; but in truth he is only thinking how best to cut it up in order to make floorboards, for his dirty feet.

Any step can take you into a neighboring galaxy; but only if you know what you might usefully do there.

Such rancid sorrows, caused by thinking that our daily hunger may be satisfied by any food we like.

Many people are in such a state of wonder that birds can fly, they think the little creatures do not need to eat.

What you pay for with money, you buy with your life.

I heard this after the death of the woman in the story, and it explained many things about her, especially the graceful movement of her understanding. She lived in an adobe house in southern Utah, not far from the rim of the Grand Canyon. It is a landscape charged with power and mystery.

....

THE COMFORT

Once upon a time a woman was walking through the forest and came upon a long, amiable, phosphorescent snake—a snake of elegance and suavity. Our friend was not well acquainted with snakes, but her attitude toward them was an extraordinary mix of fear, confusion, and ignorance: in short, that attitude so often reserved for things of rare beauty. This snake, however, was not about to be held in contempt just because he was not simple to appreciate and understand. So the snake said:

"Good afternoon. I'll bet you are terrified of me."

"I am indeed," said our terrified friend. "And don't stick your tongue out so far when you talk to me."

"You'll get used to it," said the snake.

"And why is that?" asked our friend haughtily.

"Because you are taking me home," said the snake calmly.

"I'll do no such thing," said our friend.

"Of course you will," said the snake.

And, at that, the snake floated with its satin grace over the dirt and spiraled his way up the leg of our transfixed companion. He then slipped in between two buttons of our friend's shirt, coiled slowly around her waist, above the belt, and nestled there close to the skin. In just such a superb position he fell peacefully asleep.

An hour later, when our friend's heart had left off its frenzy of pounding, she decided she had no choice but to return home. She found, on the way, how unexpectedly pleasant was the dry and delicate brush against her of the scales of the sleeping snake. And she was intrigued, even a little moved, that the snake trusted her enough to fall asleep. It would be simple to seize the snake and dash his head against a rock. But she did not do so.

So began an unruly transformation. Our friend lived continually and comfortably with the snake, who hid in clothes and in briefcases among the papers and computers and photographs. Sometimes he would lie along the woman's arm as she sat at her desk and wrote letters. Sometimes, when she was on her feet talking to her colleagues or waiting for a subway, the snake would stretch out along the length of her spine and lay his scaly head at the base of her skull. Other times, the snake would resume his favorite place—curled around our friend's waist, from where he might occasionally put his head out between two shirt buttons, to gaze about. No one save our friend ever noticed the trick; and, if they did, they denied the reality of their perception, since no woman would carry around inside her shirt a sightseeing reptile.

Later on, the snake, as it happened, saved the woman's life. She had suffered a terrible gash in an accident, the wound became infected with a rare and virulent bacteria, and the infection had spread through her body. As she was beginning her final decline, the snake moved across her skin—and entered the unhealed gash. The infection, which had resisted the most potent medicines, was vanquished by the snake's clear venom. The snake moved on, deep within the woman, among the tissues and organs, rooting out her sickness, clearing away rank pain, working a restoration. So sick was the woman that even her bones had been infected. One can imagine the effect on our friend's ideas and dreams as the snake, bringing life, moved slowly through the center passages of bone after bone.

Our friend, restored to bountiful good health, lived her life to the wild and secret benefit of the world. When death came, she did not regard it with the usual mixture of fear, confusion, and ignorance so often reserved for encounters of rare beauty. And so, while her apparent death was desperately mourned, the truth was that she did the natural and obvious things: her spirit curled round the waists of tornadoes, lay along the arms of tropical winds, moved through passages within the body of earth.

No one noticed the den of snakes that thrived near her grave.

Told to me by a hitchhiker I picked up in Paradox, Colorado. When I asked her where she was going, she replied: "I'm not sure. Where are you going?" Her question delighted me, and she rode with me all the way to Chicago. We swapped tales all those many hours. She was full of speculations. At one point she said, in her offhand way, "Sometimes I can't help but wonder whether tragedy is a durable literary form only because men never tire of trying to ennoble their violence and imbecility."

Every now and again, I still get a postcard from her.

. . . .

THE SPECIALIST IN TRUTH

Once there was a woman who lived in the backcountry of the American West. She was skillful in many different kinds of activities. She did mechanical work with automobiles, and she could read Sanskrit, as well. She could milk a cow and do calculus. She could sail a boat, and she knew the names of all the families of flowering plants. But however efficiently and happily our friend studied, or worked at different tasks, it seemed that her ignorance increased at a faster rate than her knowledge. What was worse, she was compelled to practice unremittingly both her old and her newly learned skills, and review the whole stock of information she had acquired; all as if she were burdened with a child always growing, but never growing up.

After considering these difficulties, one bright morning this woman decided to abandon her way of life and become a specialist in truth. Such a profession is not common, and because in the time our friend lived, there was (as usual) an infinite supply of truth, but little demand, the pay was very low. But our friend countenanced these hardships because sometimes the pay was so low it made her wealthy, and because her career was successful by the most old-fashioned standards of worldly accounting; that is, it was recognized by coyotes, and accepted by her friends and by the beautiful afternoon thunderheads.

It must be said that this change in real work did not result in any apparent change in her labors. She still traveled about the country and took whatever job was at hand, and she always had many choices, because she could do so many things. But her real work was contained secretly within her apparent work, just as the branching network of human veins, if understood aright, contains the river systems of continents.

And so did she live, practicing her specialty. When, for example, she repaired a car, she would make certain to align her work with the real necessities of the car's owners. One time she overhauled an engine so that it would break down precisely two years later, stranding in a small country town a man and woman who, having there the time and one another alone, finally gave themselves up to love. They were meant one day to find out more than just the nature of sweetness, but what is more essential—to find out where sweetness is meant to lead us.

Another time our friend went to work on a cattle ranch and in the course of building and mending fences created patterns of wire and wood so dazzling that the old ranch couple were visited by an unfathomable joy. It was as if the land they loved had written a letter to them, at last. They broke out the whiskey, invited over their friends, clicked glasses, and rollicked all night; and thereafter the whole community lived in such a way as to make their houses in later years honored among mountains.

These effects, of course, were not generally observed, and so our friend was able to live free of the fanfare of other people's attention, and move about at her liberty. Once for a joke, while teaching science in high school, she described the equation for the chemical transformation that created jewels in the earth; then she showed how the selfsame formula could be used to describe the coming of clarity and beauty to a conversation between friends. And she developed another set of equations, for stories and poems, that allowed her students to calculate the velocity of a text in the direction of paradise. This work will become the foundation of a new science in the humanities, to be known as the vector calculus of eschatology.

From this manner of working, she concluded that to get ahead in the world, it is only necessary that the world get ahead in your understanding. Or to put it another way, to be a specialist in work, it is necessary that your work, whatever its form, make you a specialist in all the cardiac proprieties and secret generosities. To put it another way, we are all on the payroll of this planet, or to put it another way—there's another way.

Told to me by an investment banker in New York City. She lives in a raucous tumult of numbers and commerce, yet she seemed always to take the long view, and play the long game. There is some way that, for her, facts unfold in space, and so a single data point is never isolated; it is, rather more like the aleph, the point that holds the entire universe.

We were talking about money and death.

....

THE LETTERS EVERY DAY

Once there was a busy woman who was a banker and a merchant. Day after day she watched over accounts, made loans, analyzed the social and economic evolution of the time, and presided over the labor of hundreds of her fellows. All the while, she was adjudging the quality of the goods she traded, keeping in her head information she needed to ascertain just prices, and calculating the most opportune times of participation in the markets. During all this high industry, she received many letters on business matters, some of which influenced crucially her decisions.

It was in midlife, at the height of her powers, that she began receiving letters that bore no return address.

These carefully sealed mailings, of elegant stationery, carried on the face of an envelope her address (correct even when she was traveling, and even after she had changed her post box); and, inside, a single sheet of paper folded precisely, but bearing upon it not a single word. Day after day, wherever she was, she received these extraordinary mailings amidst the analyses and solicitations, bills, remittances, friendly words, challenges, numbers, and summaries.

At first she was mildly irritated, and tossed out daily the blank, remarkable, unexpected letters. But as time went on she was visited by an inclination to save them, and, as her affairs began truly to prosper, she placed them, one by one, in a locked drawer in her private office. And she began to look forward to the arrival of these letters, lying there correct and undisturbed in the fever of correspondence. Finally, one day, at the end of an especially mercurial period of trading, she began to read them.

She began to read them after she conceived the idea that just as there are many kinds of letters, there are many ways of reading. And just as it was necessary, by the use of vision, to understand a letter, so she needed now, by the use of understanding, to envision a letter. The trouble is that understanding—the clear, unified, direct perception of reality—usually has no open place to work with full potency, no place not already congested thickly by the commotion of human affairs—our days full of appointments, air full of smoke and noise, letters full of words.

Beset as she was, she understood that the blank letters presented to her a field where another kind of idea could appear, informed by that which is blessed beyond language. That is, following an old pattern of learning, she revisited the source of language, a place where language is clear because it is pure understanding; and she changed herself. She brought her literacy to its natural conclusion: she began to read the original words, from which all the others are derived: they are to ordinary words as the foaming and moonstruck ocean is to a quiet forest pond.

Such ability brought indescribable changes to this woman's practical life. Suffice it to say that she began to work for subtle, certain, far-reaching purposes, and wielded her uncanny authority according to more playful, almost musical rules. In addition to the many businesses she analyzed, she came to study another kind of enterprise, more unified, of more worldly scope and reference—call it the enterprise of sunlight. So it was she came to concentrate her labors, in hopes of learning a work that would always be hers.

After her death, the man who administered her estate was surprised to find among her effects, in a locked drawer of her desk, many letters that seemed to be perfectly blank, but that were nonetheless creased and worn by the hands of a woman, folded and refolded, indented along the edges by the vigor of her grip. Some of them, especially the ones received toward the end of her life, showed few signs of having been handled—as though they had been opened with infinite care and longing.

So few knew the truth; everyone remembered her joy.

Cool in a summer dress, I choose
From among heaped piles of books.
Reciting poems in the moonlight, riding a painted boat . . .
Every place the wind carries me is home.

—Yu Xuanji (9ᴛʜ C)

⁓

O wind, do not stop—
My little boat of raspberry wood
Has not yet reached the Immortal Islands.

—Li Qingzhao (12ᴛʜ C)

⁓

Those that are worthy of Life are of Miracle,
for Life is Miracle, and Death, harmless
as a Bee, except to those who run—

—Emily Dickinson, in a letter to her sister

⁓

I will not serve God like a laborer, in
expectation of my wages.

—Rabia el-Adawia (8ᴛʜ C)

⁓

PART II

Told to me in Boston, at dinner near the sea, by an elusive woman I had known for about a month. The storyteller, as it turned out, if she was willing to go with you to some solitary place at night, played the flute and spoke so clearly that it was as if one could see starlight through her phrases. I had found out just how much she loved candlelight, but until she told me this story, I did not fully understand why.

···

CANDLETALK

Once upon a time a woman in her study lit a tall candle and found to her surprise that it did not, as she expected, spread a uniform light around the room. The candle, in fact, would sometimes cast all its light in a particular direction, at other times flash rhythmically, as though to some unheard music; and occasionally it would illuminate itself only. All this contrary behavior, needless to say, gave our friend the willies; but her curiosity prevented her from throwing away the truculent column of wax.

One night after the little candle had done all sorts of eerie tricks—shooting light playfully about, putting itself out and bursting back again into flame, and twirling on its stand (our friend half-expected it to sit down and read the newspaper), it seemed like the time had come to address a question to this strange light-maker.

"Well," she said, clearing her throat (for she had never before conversed with a candle), "tell me, why don't you behave yourself?"

"Well," said the candle mockingly, "why don't you? You took me into your study days ago and finally you say a word to me! Never mind that it is only to ask a rude question, at least you are showing some signs of being a human. It's about time. I was afraid I had been purchased by a bread fungus or something."

"I beg your pardon," said our friend, incensed at being reprimanded by a candle. "It's you who are rude. How can I read by a light like yours, running all over the room like a dog? And what thanks do I get for giving you a home here with me—none at all, none at all—you do whatever you please, even though you are only wax. I support you and you take advantage of me; next thing, you'll want piano lessons or something."

"If you will permit a comment from someone who is merely wax," said the candle with dignity, "there is more to candlelight than you know, and the more you know, the better we will get along. You should consider yourself on notice that I associate only with the knowledgeable among you."

And so, far into the night, and confronting by the way a number of the most humdrum matters of beauty and work, of mind and body, of light and the strategies of light, our friend and her candle debated, insulted, entreated, cajoled, taunted one another, and generally had a high time; until they felt enfolded in the bright sympathies of an otherworldly friendship.

She learned, as the candle burned down, that she could preserve its volubility and intelligence by using its flame to light another candle. By such care, she kept her little companion alive.

So it was that, by such bemused partnership, our friend continued her life with a rare sense of participation. Sometimes the candle flame would lead her to shape her ideas differently—she could, for instance, test the quality of her ideas by adjudging how exactly they fit in stencils of light the candle provided. Sometimes the candle would fall across volumes in her library whose contents bore importantly on her preoccupations. When it was more proper to greet the stars than remain indoors, the candle would dim to a mere brushstroke of light, until our friend had gone out and made the necessary salutations. Best of all, the candle sometimes spread a curtain of flame across the room, and when she drew aside that curtain, she was able to see visions of great practical value, which taught her many eccentric skills. For example, she learned how to walk the earth at night and turn the slow voltage of messages she received from the soil into prophecies useful and electric in the morning. She learned also how to discover and use her knowledge of the future, yet keep herself anonymous; so that, when terrible perils were turned aside by means of her foresight, she never was disrupted by people coming around to be grateful.

It amused our friend that some folks she knew took pride in thinking the course of their lives resulted from their own decisions, their personal strategies, the rightful imposition of their will on the world. Especially funny to her now was an idea held dear by many of them—the idea that just humankind, and not each thing in this world, is alive.

A securities attorney in Palo Alto, California, told me this story over a glass of wine. I knew she had worked with many remarkable entrepreneurs, but I had no idea how far afield some of her colleagues had gone. It may be that for some investors, participation in the venture capital community leads to ventures of soul, in ways that are often hidden, so that they might be more effective.

....

THE PROBLEM WITH COMMODITIES

Once there was a woman who made her living by selling places in heaven, as one would sell reserved seats. Since heaven is eternal, the interest was high; but since she could not guarantee the seats, the price was negotiable.

If she just could guarantee the seats, she felt sure of prosperity. And so our entrepreneur, who had the most detailed, outrageous aspirations, and wanted simply to do her work as well as she could, set off upon a quest to make herself the woman who could provide such assurance. After many a journey to the ends of the earth (some of which did not require her to leave her house); after talking to many a wayfarer of boisterous sagacity (even though these conversations were sometimes no more than a few whispered phrases); after reading whole skiesful of poetry, until the words on the page danced, until the words went off in a pyrotechnics of meaning (even though this is how everybody reads anyway); after taking lovers whose ministrations on clear summer days set off through her flesh prolonged and remarkable displays of heat lightning (even though this had been her habit in any case for some years); after all these ordinary efforts, she came into a calm and exact knowledge of the configuration of heaven.

Unfortunately, it proved harder than ever to sell her seats, which she could now guarantee with aplomb. Those who had spiritual interests of their own did not want her seats, because they knew she had obtained her knowledge by trying to become a better business-woman—and who could become wise with such vile and crude motivations? And others turned her away because if there was no risk in their purchases, they had no interest; it just wasn't thrilling enough. Yet others rejected her because she was an independent woman who had her own sources of wealth and life, and that angered them. But most of them turned her away because in order to purchase a guaranteed seat, they had to become more like her—focused, efficient, businesslike. This they were unwilling to do, because they had all learned long ago in school that commerce and soul have nothing to do with one another.

From these difficulties our entrepreneur came to understand the confusions in economic and metaphysical affairs, and the general decline in professionalism that resulted: people thought that buying and selling was a matter of calculation and survival, and not simultane-ously a matter of subtle reckoning and invisible purposes.

She did, incidentally, one thing even more baf-fling to her customers. Sometimes, instead of selling the seats, she gave them away—but only to those who could afford them.

A story from Eureka, Nevada. The bar mentioned is a splendid one—a place of wild coincidence and strange visitations. That is, a standard country bar in Nevada. The woman I met there later took me for a ride in her pickup truck, which she drove as if she were piloting a rocket. I expected any minute to be weightless and looking in wonder down upon the earth.

She told me that afternoon: "We live in such rancorous times. When men hear us tell of any good thing happening, they call it sentimental. Such men, of course, are doomed."

....

THE ENGINEERING OF FATE

Because of a red-tailed hawk, a worn bolt on a pickup, and a tune played on a country fiddle, I gave birth to a girl on the first day of spring.

This is my story: one day I was driving along the dusty roads of backcountry Nevada, and that was when I saw the hawk. He was riding a steady wind out of the west, still and marvelous, as if he had married the air.

As for myself, I'd been living in a line cabin, trying to restore some order to my mind. I had been happy enough, and prosperous enough, working as an engineer at the University of Nevada; but I felt some terrible, acid

shadow within. I felt as if everything was going excep-
tionally well, but that, lamentably, I was wasting my life.
My mind was losing its suppleness and its future.

I took a leave of absence, moved to the line cabin
near Eureka, and started to take my time with the world.
I finally had a chance to read, for long hours, in joy. In the
late afternoon I'd watch the sagebrush, spread out like a
fragrant coverlet upon the desert, and attend to the light
as it withdrew into the sky. I studied the coyotes. I followed the wind. I sought out the smallest insects.

It all led to that hawk. There he was, so inviting,
because of his buoyancy and blessed concentration. I
pulled over and watched, determined that I would stay
with him, as long as he was there, even if it meant that he
was waiting to fly among the stars. He hung there, gathering the grace of the blue desert sky. He looked in my
direction, I swear, then let the wind turn him around in
a long patient arc of wings and accomplished beauty. I
headed on into Eureka.

On the far side of town, at about the same time,
a car had stopped dead in a vacant stretch of road. Its
U-bolt had given out.

By the time I got to Main Street, it was too late to
do anything I'd planned. So I headed straight for a bar
on the ground floor of an old lodging house, where I
could read and take notes. I figured I'd stay late, down
a warm whiskey, and head home. I was about to leave
when an old man with a fiddle walked in and started to
play. It was a lovely old country ballad; even the smoke
in the bar wanted to stand up and slow-dance.

The young man whose car had broken down had
walked all the way into town. He happened to be nearby

just then. He was a musician, he heard the fiddle, and he came straight into the bar. And then straight up to me. I rose to dance with him. Right away, with their country smarts, the folks in the bar knew. After the seventh dance, they gave us a room. In that bed we traveled far into rough, sage-spiced country, where sweat is a form of light. The next day I took him home and we talked and made love, made love and talked, read books and walked and watched the stars—for weeks, and then months. We conceived a little girl. We will be together forever, in this world. Sometimes I think, in all the other worlds, as well.

If I had not stopped to watch the hawk, I never would have met him. If his car had not broken down, he would not have stopped at all in town. If not for the fiddle music, I would not have stayed at the bar, and he would not have entered the bar.

No one believes in destiny anymore. But this has not affected destiny itself. No one believes in beauty anymore, but the world is showing itself, beckoning us, hoping for us. No one believes in heaven on earth anymore, and so heaven is freely available.

No one believes in the old, sacred arithmetic anymore. If you add a hawk, a bolt, and a fiddle, what is the sum?

A brief story sent to me by a brilliant woman who lives on Vancouver Island in British Columbia. It seems to be about her own death. I had asked her to elaborate on her fierce declaration and urgent question: "The evil in the world has literal-mindedness as its root, its poison root. When the prophets condemned idolatry, this is what they meant. When will we learn that lesson? When?"

When in my return letter to her I inquired whether she might portray what she meant in a style with less aggressive metaphor, she asked me if I was willing to do without thumbs.

....

PENCIL

Once upon a time a woman was much perturbed by friends who took everything at face value. According to them, the meaning of all things in the world was determined by their human use, and not by their jocular, spiritous use.

According to them, a ledge in a canyon is only a place where a human can stand and look, and not the fated step that might be used by a young man to climb into the sky; not the stage where the coyotes go to give voice to the manuscripts of the sandstone; not where the lichen consult with the lowliest rocks, so to add a precise, necessary tracing to the contours of history.

The walk of a woman was only the means by which she could find her way to errands, to work, to a man; this walk of hers, there was no chance it might be her practice of a rhythm of wingbeats she will one day teach to fledgling seabirds; no chance it might be, by the marking of her steps, a celebration of the pattern, on a windy morning, of sunlight moving through the aspen; nor that it might represent, on a city street, her maternal traveling into the newly created country of her young daughter's stories.

Occasionally our friend would try to trick her friends into the admission that everything is anything but what it seems. She would point out, by way of example, the phenomenon of colors: an object has a given appearance because it absorbs wavelengths of all the colors of light, save one, which it reflects away: and that is what we see. So then, looked at aright, an object, in fact, is full of every color *except* the color it seems to be. Still, however much our friend persuaded and explained, portrayed and clarified, those around her turned all the more to their own affairs, and regarded her as possessed of a peculiar, unnerving confusion of mind. The idea that human action and vision hold something within; that what we do and see could come consciously to be part of a living pattern of events that is planet-wide and grace-giving—this idea was somehow unfathomable.

So it was that our friend, after a time, died. Or at least she seemed to die, for by following her own rules we might conclude that her death was a gesture that, seen through a prism that shows the wider vision, might be understood aright as a lucid, high-colored movement into the spectrum of another life.

Before she died, she wrote me with an old pencil, which she said was the baton of a conductor of symphonies, a flagpole where moved the colors of an invisible nation; or that it was the needle of a compass that points to a door which opens onto a treasure known, at just the right moment, to a certain reader of a certain book.

She wrote me this very account of herself, which seemed to be a story.

*I was told this in the dining car of a train going from
San Francisco to Chicago. I longed to talk at length with
the storyteller, but she was such a meditative woman
that, looking out the window of the train, she fell into
a perfect reverie where I was not welcome.*

    *Yet it is in just such reveries that, then as now, I seek to
be welcome.*

....

ORIGINAL GRACE AND
THE GLORY OF HISTORY

Some have lost their wings because they found them too
large, uncomfortable, and bizarre; some, because in use
the wings had proved rather unpredictable, as if they had
a mind of their own. Some thought it was unjust to have
imposed upon them without their consent so conspicu-
ous and intrusive a bodily feature; for others, they dis-
liked the way the wings were situated, after all, on the
back, making it hard to sit down at dinner parties—and
difficult in any case to see in a mirror, leaving the winged
creatures in undeserved anxieties about their elegance
and their readiness to fly. For yet others, they considered the wings too ungainly to allow efficient and graceful movement through the human world, with its doors,
offices and chairs, hearthstones and banquet tables.

Most of all, the wings were lost because if we accepted them as essential, we would have to do something with them. These are busy times, important work is going forth, the era is full of wealth and possibilities, each generation must have the courage to take upon itself the burdens of history. Who on earth has the time to consider the proper way to bring to the brilliant human endeavor so antiquated and embarrassing a birthright?

In all these judgments we are correct; we have our sound and supported reasons and compelling emotions. After all, what is more important to our story on earth than our own reasons and feelings, and the inalienable right of each of us to exercise the freedom to define his own individuality? It is, in fact, our individual sovereignty and dignity, our pride of place in creation, which is sacred: this, at least, after so many centuries, we have learned.

With our learning has come freedom, and freedom—the wholehearted, open expression of our lives and minds, our work and emotions—will, we know, in the long run, lead us to joy and prosperity. If this were not true, if we are not being led to just such pleasures, then tell me—for heaven's sake, tell me—who are they? Who are these men holding the ropes attached to the rings in our noses?

Candela lives in San Francisco. She is one of the reasons the city is the way it is. It has been complained recently that the city is getting less strange and more technological. But I think the technology will before long be taken over by the grace-giving strangeness of the place.

I have listened to her stories for hours. I relate these few incidents as plainly as possible. They are selected from the much more idiosyncratic variety of incidents in her life.

....

THE WAY SHE LABORED

Our friend Candela was a conventional young woman with a soul both wild and calm, both aggressive and subtle. She wanted to participate in the world as she found it, yet she felt that a simple, coarse, stupefied commitment to work could not be justified. In fact, she felt, in general, only one commitment: to tell what truth she knew by the way she lived. In this way, she thought she had a chance to make a home in this life; at least, the ghost of a chance.

In other words, she was just like you and me.

Her first job after she finished her education was the most obvious work she could conceive: she became the understudy of a minister in one of those churches that thinks that women, too, have souls. Unfortunately, she found that the minister had no direct personal experience of God, only a conviction that He might well exist, and that it was a good thing in any case to exhort people to virtue in His name.

What a surprise this was to our Candela! She had thought that having a confirmed dialog with the divine was a fixed prerequisite for such labors. Her own intercourse with God, which she undertook every year in midwinter when it was cold and she needed some of the Holy heat, spark, and jocund company, was something she thought would be very useful in her new job. But her minister, no. He just went on day after day spreading upon the faces of his congregation the marmalade of virtue. So plastered were they by the sticky phrases of the preacher that they could hardly go out in the world to honor his exhortations. For one thing, they had to wash up. What was Candela to do; how was she to get some plain God-talk into this mess?

She hit upon a plan. For the next sermon, she came straight into the church and took up a place in the pews, accompanied by a clothes rack from home, upon which she had hung most of her wardrobe. Because of our heroine's disinterest in matters of fashion, the hangers contained mostly sweatpants, denims, overalls, hoodies, and funny hats; hence, this was an easy rack to roll about.

As the pastor began one more stem-winding sermon on the necessities of virtue, Candela, in her simple way, listened with ferocity. For every one of his admonitions, she would put on another article of clothing. So numerous were the virtues suggested by her earnest compatriot that before long she had taken on the profile of the fat lady in a circus. Even the good Father could not help but notice that one of his congregation was growing. And so, not recognizing his swollen assistant, he summoned her forth.

Now Candela had to figure out how to move under such a weight of cloth. Taking courage, and slick with a downpour of sweat under her garments, she shuffled out into the nave, waddled to the front of the church, and situated herself directly in front of the pastor, who now understood that this puffy object was his own assistant. He had thought her so sweet and inoffensive. And so she proved to be!

Candela turned slowly to face the churchgoers and said:

"Everything has changed! The good Father and I have been playing tricks, and now the joke's on you!"

The pastor could do nothing because, of course, the joke was on him.

Candela went on:

"You probably think that in some story you are portrayed as having upon your face the marmalade of virtue: a sweet thing for you to savor on your day of worship. Well, that story will be wrong. The truth is, you leave this church every Sunday covered over with ideas about virtue like so many layers of clothes. You are weighed down by what you want your soul to wear. You must feel just as I feel, standing here. Yet going forth with such bulk is the very opposite of our intention; in fact, we want you to leave here naked, having stripped from yourself the ideas standing between you and this world. For virtue, rightly considered, strips away your own self; it is, in fact, the way you learn to take off the clothes of your soul. Why not see the truth about ourselves?"

The pastor, meanwhile, hearing all this improvisation, was mad as a hen.

"And now I leave you," she said with a winning smile to one and all.

"But where are you going?" asked the exasperated Pastor.

"To get naked," she answered brightly.

The next morning after her parable-in-action, she turned up as usual for work at the church, fully expecting anything from a pat on the back to unreserved huzzahs of praise. Instead, she found the Father still so mad his lips were flecked with foam, so mad he could not speak without swallowing his tongue. Seeing this, she sat quietly in hopes he would calm down. But there is a limit on how long a woman is willing to sit with a foaming man; and when someone came in and handed her a paycheck, she got the idea that her performance had not been universally acclaimed.

Yet there was good news in all this: she began to understand that she would have an increasing number of career options.

And so it has proved to be: She has worked as a risk analyst in a financial management firm, a translator of poetry from Italian and Spanish, a waitress in a jazz club, and a cook in a Moroccan restaurant, where she specialized in dishes made with pomegranates or cinnamon (both of which ingredients she used to introduce certain variations in the amorous undertakings of late evening). She has taught in a community college, specializing in the Jewish and Arab poetry of medieval Spain, and is currently engaged in the study of mushrooms and juggling.

In every single job she has proved to be magnificently indispensable. And from every single one she has been fired. She is, therefore, not in the least discouraged.

AFTER ALL, IF each of us is meant to take off the clothes of our soul, then it can only be because, looking into the mirror, we might see ourselves as we really are. And within the sorrow we know so well, within the terrible sorrow that each of us carries, because of our ignorance, because of what we have done—beyond the savagery of every day, the pandering habits of mind and our hysteria of purposes—within and beyond all that, we might find our chance.

Candela is coming to see you.

I have collected these graffiti in bars all over the American West. I caught her carving only once, and then only because she let me. I loved her so much. She could not hold on to a single gift given her, not a single one. She gave them all away again, incorrigibly, and I came to see that she was giving away her whole life, every day. She did so with a calm and potent independence.

....

GRAFFITI CARVED IN BARTOPS BY A TRAVELING GIRL

People say: where there's smoke there's fire; and by this means, many a fire has been found, after which everyone went home contented. History would have been different if they would have stayed, to see what was burning.

He thought he could hear the music of the spheres; but it was the sound of his own soul, laughing at him.

There is no creature lowlier than the professional writer, who must laboriously glue fancy veneer over the cheap and rotten wood of his life.

The woman is a genius: she paints the world that holds her as a brush.

If wildflowers do not take root in your sentences; if the homely has no luster, life looks like flesh and grass looks like grass; if the world throws money for you, and you would play fetch all your earthly years; if you think changing the world is more difficult than chang- ing your eyes—then start over. For heaven's sake, start over. Do it now.

People who cannot reminisce about the future have no memory.

This story was told to me on the Lower East Side of
New York City, by a woman who worked in a pawnshop.
Pawnshops, as everyone knows, are hives of stories. The
woman you will find here, who bought the compass, is
now a judge in New York State, known for the almost-
transcendent clarity of her judicial decisions.

....

THE COMPASS

Some years ago a woman bought a compass in an old
pawnshop. She was attracted to this particular compass by the elegant silverwork of the case. This case, in
the form of a pentagon, had inscribed upon it a series
of interlocking spirals that spun together and revolved
apart, gathering sunlight as they moved; it looked as if
the metal itself was set moving. These phenomena so
entranced the woman that she forgot to open the case
and look at the face of the compass before she bought it.

When she came, in good time, to do so, she was
dismayed to find on the compass face a whole eccentric series of marked orientations, rather than the usual
north, south, east, and west. What is more, the needle on
the compass changed its position in a way mischievously
unrelated to the magnetic field of the earth—rather, its

movements showed a swift, calibrated response to forces and energies otherwise undetectable to our friend. She, of course, tried to replace this bizarre instrument; but when she returned to the location of the pawnshop, she found a vacant lot.

At first, she thought she had been cheated. But she was patient with the strange ways of the world, and not excited by intrigue, nor maddened by the impractical. She decided to keep the compass with her.

Months passed. One morning, in the course of a frustrated search for some important papers, she accidentally knocked the useless instrument from her desk, and the case was wrenched open. When she picked it up, she noticed that the needle was pointing to a locked drawer. Sure enough, the lost papers were there, even though it was impossible that they should be so. At this point, however, our friend resolved not to be discouraged by simple impossibilities.

Her compass turned out to have all sorts of uncanny properties. Sometimes in a meeting of people it would point out an honest man, at just that time in the conversation when his clear commentary would be decisive. Sometimes it would indicate whoever knew just the joke that a gathering of people needed in order to understand their own absurdity. One time she was guided by the compass needle to the end of an alley, and through a door she found there, she entered an extraordinary forest, someplace she thought she recognized. She wandered widely, and later fell into company with a family of foxes, and learned their grace, stealth, beauties, and quickness; even as she explained to them the incurious ways of humans.

In another instance she decided to follow, without watching where she was going, the turning of the needle as she walked in her home city. When the needle began to spin, she looked up and found herself in the capital of another country, speaking another language; and thereafter she lived simultaneously in two cities at once. Eventually, she understood that the needle was meant to teach the orientation of hearts; and later she even became able to sense, without consulting her compass, which direction to follow, as she moved down the proper and magical pathways within her days.

It was about this time that while on the street of a distant city in a strange land in another time, for no reason at all she looked at the compass; the needle was pointing at an old pawnshop across the street. At once she recognized it as the same one where her adventure had begun. And upon entering the shop, she found behind the counter the same old man.

"I presume you want this back now," said our friend.

"Certainly," said the old pawnbroker. "It's time."

And he took back the compass and refunded our friend's money.

"It is a very fine compass," commented our friend, who did not know what to say.

"Yes, it is," said the pawnbroker. "People are always teaching one another how to use such instruments. This instrument, our beloved compass, teaches people how to use themselves."

"I hope someone will come soon to your shop and purchase it," said our friend.

"Oh, they will come and look," said the pawnbroker, "but it's rare indeed for anyone to buy it from me. You see, people are well educated these days. They know there are four cardinal points; they know what compasses should do. Because they know some things, they think they know everything else. And not only that, almost no one walks in here to trade and to learn; rather, they come here to have their knowledge confirmed and their personalities gratified. They come to negotiate, to see if something here attracts or excites them, to show me what they know. What they want, often, is simple—to be satisfied."

"Satisfied?"

"They leave satisfied with themselves, having proven they are wary and streetwise—too smart, for instance, to be cheated by a wily old pawnbroker with a defective compass."

Mathematics, of course, is an art both practical and sacred. And there are some new practitioners who, by moving the work forward, also recover the ancient association of numbers with a divine order. I cannot identify this mathematician by name, since she works in so dignified a profession and her reputation is one of the utmost sobriety.

She lives in Amsterdam. However, like any good scientist, she is willing to go where her work takes her. She has taught in England, Switzerland, and France. She loves Amsterdam, and told me that in her extended family tree is the artist M. C. Escher, in whose work any one line may mark both a boundary and a place of transformation.

....

MATRICES

Once upon a time there was a mathematician who specialized in matrices, which are arrangements of numbers in a coordinated order. Once put in such order, each number can be referred to by coordinates that give its location; and, what is more, one matrix can be linked up with another, of a similar type, so that a wholly new arrangement can be composed. All this, however, did not satisfy our mathematical friend, who wondered if she could put two matrices together and come up with something that wasn't even a matrix. Such speculations were typical of our mathematician, who owned an exploratory, strange, calculating, keen nature.

To try this experiment, she put into a matrix, in place of numbers, real things from the world, things for which she had a certain affinity. For example, in one matrix she put parrots, old opera capes, excellent cigarettes, and cinnamon sticks. In another she put a deck of cards, a forest, bread, and a bicycle.

Then, with the superb precision for which mathematicians are known, she fitted the matrices together to see what would come of it. And sure enough, right there in her study, she saw before her on the paper of her calculations, as in a vision, herself. She was in the forest practicing a bewildering yet harmonious series of circus tricks: wearing an opera cape, with a parrot on her shoulder, she did card tricks and smoked a cigarette with great relish, all as she rode around on a bicycle; only then to leap from the bicycle and begin to juggle cinnamon sticks.

Never had she felt so exuberantly mathematical. But yet, delighted as she was, she was puzzled not to find the bread from the second matrix; but just then from the kitchen her husband entered bearing a fragrant loaf of bread, just baked, that he meant to share with her. And, excited by her discoveries, and stimulated by the opportune tastiness of the bread, they gave themselves over to an afternoon of delectation—matrix to matrix, as it were.

Her fellow mathematicians, it is sad to note, have been slow to adopt her combinatorial techniques, and to this day prefer to set numbers, rather than the real elements of the world, into the specific order of matrices—an order, we now know, so ripe for extension, for trickiness, for conjuration.

Our friend, however, working either in solitude or with her willing and delighted husband, extended her investigations. And just as she was able to produce real bread in her initial investigations, she can now, with her refined techniques, produce whole days of real events in the world.

This is all in hopes that with her work in mathematical logic—her professional concentration, of course— she'll one day be able to prove with beautiful rigor that the algebra of numbers leads naturally and inevitably to the algebra of reality.

Told on the third floor of the Pinacoteca, in Siena, Italy. The paintings are early, full of gold, with a blaze of light that can be detected from outer space. I was standing before the painting of an old Sienese master named Simone Martini, when I realized that I had someone by my side, who had stood for an equally long time, as if we participated in the same trance of beauty.

....

WHO NEEDS A LOVER

Sheila was a cook. She prepared pasta and *bistecca fiorentina*; she made bread and little *pizzetas,* sauces of Gorgonzola, and vegetables steaming and flavored with grappa. And in all these fragrant and splendid concoctions, at some point in her simmering and touching-up, her sautéing, marinating, blending of subtleties that makes for the exaltation of the senses, at some point, in every case she used olive oil. Now, it could be presumed that her fondness for olive oil derived from the way, at home each night, her boyfriend took some of the thick sunny liquid into his hands, smoothed it over her body, and made love to her until she glowed in the dark. But this was no more than a good cook had a right to expect. Though she admitted that it was splendid to have such a lover, still—the movement of light she felt within her days did not come from pleasure alone. It came from her certainty that she was doing the work she was born for, that her work would lead her somewhere; that cooking and love lead somewhere.

So the months passed. It was in early June, and, one day when she was in the storeroom, just about the time she was coming to the end of her stock of olive oil, she noticed the old bottle standing on the floor, in the corner. It was a tall graceful bottle, of clear, handmade, firm brilliant glass, and it looked to her as if it had been there forever. The oil inside was dense dark gold.

It seemed too good to cook with, so she took it home—which, as it turned out, was a lucky thing. Because that night, when she and her lover lay together with a sweat upon them both hot and cool, both sweet and salt, as they lay in bright thankfulness for the chance to love, for every detail of the world—in this state, they noticed that the adjoining room was crazy with light.

She had left the old bottle of olive oil in there.

Now, an inexplicable luminosity undid the dark of the night, though it seemed in its ripe strangeness like a natural phenomenon. Of course, neither of them was in the mood, not to mention the posture, to make a practical investigation of the light. And so, in each other's arms, they ventured into sleep.

In the morning, they went and found the bottle exactly where she had left it—standing there, plain, golden, quiet.

Next night, though, the same thing happened. And when, this time, they bestirred themselves to look, they saw in darkness the bottle of olive oil embraced with light, possessed by light; they saw within the glass a steady, perfect, tawny incandescence.

Back in bed, the two of them took counsel and decided that it would take a summer of lovemaking to figure out this mystery. And in that conclusion, they were wholly correct. For during all the cool black hours that summer the oil shone with a play of light that brightened softly all their house and all their lives. And by summer's end, at the autumnal equinox, they knew enough to wait; and just as they thought, the house held its darkness all through the night.

And that was how they found out that in this world, each thing may be enamored, may have its match, may make its union.

And that was how they found out that when there is shining, then there is loving.

And that was how they found out that olive oil has a lover: the light of summer.

This set of sayings was given to me by an unusual writer who seeks, and publishes, anonymously, statements that come from years of revision of her manuscripts. Some of the lines here were, at one time, whole novels. One conversation with her was worth a novel.

She lives in London, where she is a distinguished leader of a technology firm. None of her colleagues are aware of her novels and her proverbs. They are aware of her insistence on concision.

....

SHE REVISED HER STORIES UNTIL THEY BECAME PROVERBS

Every gem was once a rock—and still is.

The musculature of a man, perhaps; but does he have the bones to support any such strength? The brain of a man, perhaps, but . . .

First foundations, and hope; even if, especially if, we cannot recognize a wall.

So skilled at following maps, he never left home.

Nobody believes in flying carpets, except secretly, in the privacy of their own homes, where the carpets are.

We buy hammers, who would not recognize a nail.

He was afraid of bees, so he thought honey was bitter.

A man who never went out of doors, because he was sure the sun was looking at someone else.

The lighthouse, which warns of rocks, is probably made of them.

A doctor in Dallas, Texas, told me this one recently. I met
her in the intensive care unit and noted the grace and feroc-
ity of her concentration. She refused to talk about the story
afterward. I felt, in her presence, a kind of cleansing fear.

And it made me think once again about how it seems
always to be true, that in order to have and wield real
power, a woman has to have the skills to conceal, when
necessary, that very power.

....

BEAUTIFUL DOCTOR OF FAITH MEETS THE JANITOR

I never expected that I would meet so handsome a doctor. Even before I had begun my work as the office cleaning lady, I had heard of him. He was a graceful man with
dark hair and large soft brown eyes. I thought that it
was unusual that he would want to interview a cleaning lady, but one evening, there I was, alone with him in
his expensive offices. He asked me many questions, but
mostly he told me about himself.

His clinic provided special services to wealthy people. He fixed their faces. But, as he explained, he took the
earnings and used them to treat the poor and the sick;
everyone, he said, should have the benefits of beauty. There
was, beginning in the afternoon, a long line of raggedly

supplicants at the back door of his office. Some of those who were admitted were examined and treated for free. Gradually, over the years, the generosity and dedication of the doctor came to public notice, which brought him even more patients, both rich and poor. What mattered to him, he said, was to be trusted by all his patients. He was a religious man, he explained, and trust in God meant, on earth, trust in the good will of a caregiver, someone who could see in each of us the divine image. Without such faith, there could be no successful treatment of the sick or the ugly. In the love and faith that moves between doctor and patient, he said, our healing begins.

Now, I must say that I thought this language a bit curious, but I needed a job. I had just finished high school in the deserts of northern Mexico, and I needed to earn some money to make my way to college.

I never started work until everyone was gone for the day. Then I cleaned everything, the rooms with their medical waste, the closets, the toilets; the scabs, the blood, the puke. I dusted the doctor's office, his books, and all the plaques, certificates, and commendations that recognized his charitable work.

One room, located just behind the doctor's office, was always locked. I was told it was a storeroom, and that I never need enter there. This injunction violated my sense of responsibility and thoroughness, but that was not what really bothered me. Not even the rustling sounds that issued from the locked room bothered me, because I knew what they were. They were the sounds of moving rattlesnakes. I had gotten to know many snakes—one might say on a first-name basis—in my home desert. I came to love them, and I knew what they

sounded like. There were at least a hundred thick diamondbacks in that room.

It didn't seem like something I could ask about. But
I didn't want to, especially since I never saw the doctor, except now and then: I would be cleaning and suddenly know I was not alone. I'd turn, and there he'd be,
standing silently, watching me. Then he'd tell me that
he needed to retrieve the file of a patient, or prepare an
emergency medication for someone.

I figured I could understand more if I came into the
office on one of my nights off. I knew that once a month
the doctor would gather with his friends in his office. I
cleaned up the cigar butts. So on the night I thought I'd
find them, I hid myself in a big ventilation duct, so that I
could look out through the vent into the doctor's office.
If you want to know the best hiding places, ask your
cleaning lady.

The first thing I noticed was the physical perfection
of the men who gathered in the office. They all, I believe,
had been patients, and there was a glossiness to them, a
fixed symmetry of features, all wonderfully angled and
shaped, and overall a sense of fitness and bounteous
good health. They positively shone, as though covered
with some imported, precious salve.

The doctor touched a button, and the material on
the wall behind his desk folded back. Behind the material was another wall, this one of glass. It allowed us all to
see the room full of diamondbacks. The room, except for
the side that was the window, had walls made of mirrors.
As I watched, the doctor rose, left the room, and returned
with a patient whom I knew he had operated on that day.
Slowly, with his sure touch, he took the bandages off;

and he told the patient that he thought the surgery had gone fine, and he was eager to bring him before a mirror.

All the beautiful men in the room were holding their stomachs, trying to restrain a boom of laughter. The patient was disfigured ingeniously. His nose was a piece of purple rubble. His ears were sacks of flesh that swung as he staggered around the room. His teeth had all been pulled. His eyes were bleeding smudges; his eyelids had been snipped off so that he could not blink. All of his skin was scaly, bruised, suppurating. It looked like the hide of a beaten, dying iguana.

With a reassuring whisper, the doctor pushed his patient into the room of snakes. The patient saw his face in all the mirrors, reflected over and over; then he saw the doctor watching with his friends. He screamed fiendishly, until blood bubbled out of his throat. The snakes moved slowly toward him, as if trained. They followed him as he ran around the room, molten with horror, slamming absurdly into the mirrors. Because he kicked the snakes, and stamped on them, they struck him, starting with his legs. It took quite a while. As the man weakened, finally a few got their fangs in his face. The doctor and his friends watched him swell with poison and hatred; and then die in rampant agony.

They burst into applause.

The next day, I gave my notice of departure. The doctor wanted to do what he called an exit interview. I was eager to leave, but I thought I was owed an explanation. When I recounted to the doctor all I had seen of his nighttime show, he was completely calm. He said:

"I am a good and pious man. Everyone knows this. My friends and I, we have a position of exceptional responsibility in the world. By the beauty of our faith, reflected in our own beauty, we are inspired to carry out our obligations to society. We are, to state it plainly, the men to restore the world. We cannot allow these—call them the doubters—to deride our good works. If you do not admire us, you attack us. If you have no faith in our goodness, then you mock us. The man you saw was disrespectful of me; he offered no thanks at all, no openhearted adoration of the chance he had, here with us. We were not angry. But this is behavior we cannot permit. We must show such a man how, at last, history is ours. We make them face justice, which is ours because of our beauty."

I did not reply; I just walked over to the room with the snakes and wrenched it open. I used the low, long whistle I learned in the desert that makes a diamondback fall asleep. Then I gathered all the snakes into three big cleaning bags. The doctor did not raise his voice, but I thought there was a small glint of panic when he said:

"You must be a witch—"

Which, of course, had some truth in it. I was the daughter of a tribal healer who still knew some of the plain sorcery of my people. I went over to the doctor and touched his soft, handsome face. He was, no doubt, used to such a touch from women. But mine is different. I have a touch that turns people, as it were, into themselves; they show themselves helplessly. For example, I touched one young woman, and everyone could see the wild playfulness in her, her grace and swiftness: briefly she had the body and poise of a gazelle. Then she resumed her womanly countenance, full of light.

When I touched the doctor, his head changed shape, into the blunt, short snout of a scorpion. The dull black eyes fit well. The thick, plated neck looked odd coming from the white collar of his doctor's coat. Overall, though, the scaly body he now sported gave him a certain rough grace.

For him, and to him, I gave the form he would have until his death.

He could not rise from his chair, of course. He fell forward onto his desk. His huge arching tail with its fearsome stinger curled behind him impressively, swaying there.

When I left, I heard the scuttling of his feet, as if he were trying to learn to walk with his new set of legs. Perhaps he was grateful that I was leaving his office in such a splendor of cleanliness. Or perhaps he knew the repugnance that would rise in all who would see him, in the hours before he was slaughtered and exhibited.

At least he was moved to say goodbye. I assume this was because he recognized that he looked better than ever.

I LET THE snakes go in the desert. They, in fact, were beautiful, once in their homeland. They will live and recover, thrive and evolve through the many worlds.

The doctor who abused them will, after his death, have to confront the snakes he imprisoned and everyone he tormented and killed. Then he will die for all time.

I did, by the way, make enough money to start my university studies. And in my current work in the medical arts, I have no real use for my magical capacities. Just yet.

In southern Tunisia, at the edge of the Sahara, near the town of Ksar Ghilane, there is an old Roman fort, which looks out over the sands. It marks the end of an empire. In that ruined turret of stone, near dusk, in the light breeze, I heard this story from a Persian traveler who hoped someday to return home. She knew by heart long passages from Omar Khayyam and Hafiz.

....

THE JACKAL AND THE BUTTERFLY

There are those who think the jackal is mean-spirited and lazy, capering irresponsibly over the dunes of unknown deserts to eat the remains of other animals. The jackal herself, though, is known to feel this opinion unjust, since by her opinion she is just giving herself to her assigned role in the theater of nature; and so, she says, we may judge her only if we know the play as a whole.

One day a desert traveler and a jackal were discussing this matter, when it was resolved by a butterfly. The conversation went like this:

"Now, jackal," said the fascinated traveler, "you must admit that you do not represent for us any ideal of character. In fact, even to think of you impairs the dignity of any of us who hope to refine our intelligence, to develop in ourselves capacities of openness and honesty. You live by tooth and muscle, stealth and trickery, scavenging and appetite. Such is your destiny. And so must we part ways."

"Wait just a minute," said the jackal in her hasty, scurrilous way. "I may have the qualities you mentioned. But they are in truth advantages; and you must consider whether they might be useful beyond your slothful imaginings. What if it is my destiny today to serve you and your kind? Is it not possible that I need my teeth to dispose of the dead, the better to do service to the curious and lively among you? I needed muscles to speed me to your side and to hold you here, fascinated by the poise and grace of my movement. I needed stealth in my approach to the angel of Death, since I have taken upon myself the task of outwitting him on your behalf."

"You talk just like a jackal," said our traveler. "You twist your words with strange wit, and your rhetoric, your speed, your intentions, they are all at the mercy of your jackal's nature. You understand the qualities of a person and then use that understanding to take advantage of him. You saw, for instance, that I was curious about you, and that I liked to talk, and so have you lured me into conversation."

"And you," said the jackal, "contort your words with the logic of a human, who, in his human way, sees everything in relation to himself, and to his ideas of what the world is like. You think you know what a virtue is, what a fault is: you presume, first of all, that they are qualities belonging to humans, rather than belonging to the world. You think the world is about you. But in fact, none of us moves according to our own script. We must change our role according to events—according to the propositions the world makes to us every minute. Now, will you continue on with me?"

There was an ominous rumble up ahead, and the jackal looked steadily at her interlocutor.

"What on earth was that?" said our alarmed traveler.

"A landslide," said the jackal. "Will you come with me?"

"Why should I?" asked the traveler suspiciously.

"Because without my company you will be lonely," said the jackal. "All your companions were killed by the tonnage of rocks that has fallen upon them. This accident would not have happened but for one of your fellow travelers, who went scrambling up an unstable hillside after an extraordinary butterfly. Butterflies, as all you humans know, represent lightness of spirit, beauty, grace, and liberation."

And, as the two of them went together along the road, the traveler saw that the jackal had spoken the truth. In despair of his dead companions, he screamed, "Why didn't you warn us?"

"I tried. For I saw the butterfly, and the hillside; and I knew the danger. I spoke in your language, appealing to everyone in your group as they passed. But you were the only one who would stop to answer me. All the others saw no use in talking with a disreputable jackal, when they could pursue instead an unforgettably beautiful butterfly."

"My dead friends!" exclaimed our poor traveler.

"Do not worry," said the jackal, "I have use for them."

"And what is that?"

"I am going to eat them," said the jackal.

"Just like a jackal," said the man in disgust.

"Of course," said the animal. "I could not save them, as I was able to save you, because of your generous and honest curiosity. But I am sure that, now dead, and therefore wiser than previously, their spirits would be glad of their bodies nourishing the jackal."

"What is the worth of any learning?" asked our friend in his bitterness and sorrow.

"Besides," the jackal went on happily, "given the human weakness for ignorant admiration, and with all those butterflies fluttering around in the world, being splendid and free, it is important I be well fed, and follow my subtle and disreputable ways. That way, at least some of you will have a chance to find salvation."

Told by another investment banker in London, a woman of almost mythic competence and courtesy. Before she told me this story, she had been describing in the most searching and serious detail her readings of the early stories of Kafka and her interest in the Sufi saint Bahaudin Naqshband.

I told her that I could hardly believe some of the work she described in her story, and she answered: "No one, no one at all, cares if you believe. But you should consider whether you can watch, and listen, and develop the patience to study our lives. If you can learn what we do, you just might have your chance."

....

A BUSINESS LIFE,
A SOCIAL LIFE

Once upon a time a well-known, prosperous woman awoke to discover, alarmingly, that she had a rare skin disease. The skin on her right hand had become completely transparent. For a moment she felt a horror at the exposed complication of blood vessels, the crisscrossed luminous padding of muscles, the mysterious nerves, the tracery of finely fitting bones. But as she watched, that horror evaporated beneath the natural sunlight of her amazement.

This woman, our friend, had that very morning to affix her signature to documents, comprising the formal agreement of a long-negotiated financial matter. But when she took up a pen to sign, she was struck by the musical shiftings, the painted and precise alteration of bone, muscle, and nerve, and she could not concentrate on her task. In fact, no one else could either, for the business colleagues of our friend had been overmastered by their own fascination. It was as if a treasure chest had been opened, and all the jewels knew one another, and had for millenniums been looking forward to this performance together in the light.

None of the colleagues present could resist asking for some special trick of the hand. One wanted to see our friend pick up a paper weight and put it down again. The kaleidoscopic effects of this trick alone were such that it had to be repeated several times. Another trick was the drumming of fingers on the tabletop, which created a shifting of colors, as though the light had been invigorated by prisms. Someone else wanted to see a slow-motion snapping of the fingers, a spectacular trick that made it look like a tropical storm at sunrise was forming in our friend's newfound palm.

The favorite trick of all was the slow unfolding of the fist into the fully opened hand. And of course they all hoped they would be able to see her fingertips move across the keyboard of a piano.

After a few weeks of tricks, and much conversation with her colleagues, our friend remarked that everyone's hand had the same qualities, and that the fact of hands is not less wondrous, for being concealed. She noted as well that if we conceive of the earth itself as a hand holding all our lives, and having greater resources for wonder than our own mere bones and veins, that it may very well be worthwhile to look more carefully and patiently at our own planet. It, of course, was not covered, except by the crude and rough skin of human conception.

Everyone agreed that the analogy was an important one, and they made a pact to take the rest of their lives to find out what the world really was like. It was the obvious and necessary thing to do. That was seven years ago.

Some of her friends now do various kinds of work, all of it having to do with the real, often invisible world that we all talk about occasionally, before we return to our pressing individual affairs. If I might describe one of the most improbable and complex of these labors: one of them, using techniques she has refined over many contemplative years, melts down opals and combines them with the fluid song of certain meadowlarks. To this brew she adds a clear solution made of small portions from each of the headwaters of many rivers and a liquor made from traditional distillations of twilight; and then she gently paints the resulting mixture on the hearts of young girls. It sends them off in the direction of incandescent adventures.

Another of them is a teacher. He teaches children how to watch, on windy afternoons, the strong patterns of flashing along the broad lines of cottonwoods, so that they might be better able to recognize the bright pathways in their own lives.

Another of the friends has taken on a job of courier of moonlight, and in the middle of the day delivers satchels to certain people. She does this for those who know how to use moonlight to lend to their work, their ideas, and their language certain lunar qualities: softness; suggestiveness; lucent, lovely variability; and power— for example, the ability to make whole oceans move.

The others have different jobs. We could describe them, but you have yourself been witness to what they do; they all collaborate, and their accomplishments are everywhere.

You may ask, in the meantime, what work is being done by our friend, who started all this philosophical tomfoolery. She has the simplest work of all—just going about her business and shaking hands with everyone she sees. After all, she has bonds to sell, companies to analyze, economists to bedevil. Shaking hands seems like a traditional part of daily etiquette, until people see the hand they have in theirs. As a matter of fact, it *is* part of daily etiquette; our friend always was a convivial and mannerly woman, and it is natural to her to conceive that the most commonplace courtesy, honestly undertaken, might lead us directly to an extraordinary new life. It all goes to show something that she had often thought—that the mundane may be inevitably a matter of spirit; and that, in all our conduct, what is most in harmony with miracle is good manners.

This ornate and outlandish story was told to me in Utah,
where they have the roughest bars. The woman tending
bar had a front tooth missing, and on her hip a mysteri-
ous, beautiful tattoo, octagonal in shape. When I looked
at her, she could hold my gaze, even from the far end of
the bar, and even as she was mixing a drink.

I wondered later if she used hallucinogenic drugs. But
she told me that she lived a life of absolute sobriety, so as
to have the best chance to participate intelligently in the
world we had made together, which was a kind of collec-
tive hallucination.

....

IN PRAISE OF FEMALE BARTENDERS

Our friend, a sampler of spirits, was sitting at a bar. He noticed that one of the bottles in the rack was empty. This empty bottle, however, still had a pouring spout and was placed in company with the whiskey, rum, and other spirits frequently used. When the bartender was asked why an empty bottle merited such treatment, she answered that the bottle contained the bar's home brew, the only bottle of that unique beverage ever prepared.

Our friend in his amusement asked for a straight shot of the brew. To his surprise, the bartender, in her meticulous way, tipped the empty and worn bottle over a shot glass and poured nothing into it. Our friend paid, and then, not knowing what else to do, lifted the glass to his lips and drank the liquor it did not contain, tasted the spirit he had not perceived, swallowed notions he had not expected, and felt himself ready to enter wholeheartedly into a life he had hardly dared hope for.

All around, he could perceive the earthly powers he always had dreamed about; and, comically enough, these powers now approached him, addressed him, and welcomed his questions. The change was simple to describe: what had seemed to be separate forms of life or matter, alien, distant, and aloof—say, for example, plants, weather, or rocks—these very forms now became close, friendly, and helpful.

To state it even more simply: everything took on its own true life. The parts played in our history and destiny by the things of earth, he could understand. Everything showed itself to him; and he to them. And the bartender grinned.

First, the two men next to him at the bar revealed to him that they were not men at all, but rather two date-palm trees that had taken on human form. And why would they have done so? So they could discuss with him secrets of life known to palm trees, such as how to be dignified and life-giving among sand dunes in harsh and deadly climates. In addition, as the conversation drifted on, they clarified for him how palm fronds in the desert, on midnight of the spring equinox when there is a full moon, will glisten in a way to direct your gaze to a certain evening star. If you watched this star calmly all evening, and if you were honest, you would be able from then on to prophesy.

This was surprising news. But more was to come—
an energetic woman burst into the bar: she turned out,
really against all the odds, to be, though he could hardly
believe it, a volcano. She bought him another drink and
told him stories, including some funny ones about men
who had not thought her formidable and nearly had
to suffer incineration. As their musings took on more
confidence, she tutored him helpfully on how he might
reach deep into the earth to encounter molten currents,
so to bring into use common materials that, set out in
the open air, give light.

A sunflower taught him how his life could move in
easy and gradual concert with the hours of the day. And,
as our friend began to drink more heavily, a cyclone (she
had a muscular form and startling white hair) turned
up and was very glad to meet him, and spoke at length
to him. In fact, a sympathy and a hopefulness moved
between them, and such was the vigor and depth of their
exchange that when the cyclone took the hand of our
friend, there was in that handshake of newfound friendship a concentrated, glittering circulation of power.

Our friend, as we may well imagine, continued to
drink. And he saw how all the varieties of life might, if
we would seek to be useful, come closer to us. To his
considerable astonishment, a shark, dressed in a rather
natty suit, stopped in, and showed him how to stream-
line his thoughts so that their swiftness of movement
had always a fierce, attentive grace. Finally, at the end
of the day, someone put in his hand some freshly cut
sugarcane, and as he closed his fingers upon it he learned
how to make his bones like sugarcane, so that the mar-
row sweetened his blood, and he could walk forth onto

the road that led to the lover he would then be ready to embrace. And he felt that he might have some chance to be worthy of such embraces.

When our friend was able to pause amid the common and happy shenanigans of this education, he recalled how all this had started with a certain beverage. He inquired of the bartender what processes were used in brewing such a spirit, and what rules of etiquette pertained to its consumption. She replied that any honest request for the beverage would bring a sufficient quantity into existence. Most people simply were not willing to seek the brew, in such a way that it could be found. For example, they did not usually believe it might be found in their homely neighborhood bar. But it happens to be the case that it is the function of bars everywhere, she said, to provide a home brew. All the other spirits are stocked simply to give us a taste for the real thing.

Now, said the bartender, the empty vessel represents of course the customer himself; and he must recognize this, and drink deeply. A customer, however, who thinks himself full will not notice the empty bottle; and so he takes some other drink. Many bartenders, unbelievably, have not even heard of the home brew; and so they see no vessel full of world-spirit, but only an empty bottle to be chucked into the rubbish bin.

"A desperate situation," said our friend.

"Indeed," said the bartender, as she winked at him. "The only consolation is that so many people are being driven to drink."

Anisetta attended Amherst College in Massachusetts. Sometimes, in her dreams, Emily Dickinson would appear and kiss her on the nose. A young man gave me this account with the most carnal and spiritous enthusiasm, and then wept with his eyes open.

This is one of the few stories in this collection I heard from a man; I include it because it is about a woman whose role in his life was transformative and unforgettable.

....

THE THANK-YOU NOTES

Our friend Anisetta was raised to write thank-you notes: no kindness, no hospitality, no gift was received by our intrepid young woman but was acknowledged promptly by a note checkered with suitable effusions.

As Anisetta grew older and made her way in the world, she noticed the things we all notice: that society was a holocaust of broken promises; that hatred ran here and there like molten rock, blowing off steam through volcanoes and people; and that ignorance, always in a devouring mood, was nourished only by human souls. She noticed also that, despite everything, we all have a chance: with a little wariness, with some no-nonsense striding into the midst of things, with the will to send phrases like falcons to circle her adversaries, with the natural momentum of heaven given to women, and with unladylike cantankerous maneuvering and a good education: with these things, a woman could find her way into the midmost of the world—there to have her celebrations.

Now, by the time she hit the university, Anisetta was not one to keep mum when a celebration was called for. After all, she loved so many things. She loved particle physics, theology, gin, diesel mechanics, and sexual pleasure. She had good teachers, and a long strong boyfriend named Dominico, who loved to take her home for a lunch of honey, muffins, and sharp cold cider, after which she would take him into a rumpled old brass-framed bed, happily situated under the sky- light. And there together they would form long series of integral equations: integrals, as we all know, take con- stant practice, and must be done with patient, search- ing attentiveness.

As the seasons turned, their mathematical exper- tise increased.

It was at this unlikely juncture in her life that Anisetta remembered the etiquette of thank-you notes. After all, so much was going on, she had to have a way of keeping track. And so she began sending her notes very promiscuously, to wit: she began thanking people not just for their kindnesses, but for their barbarities.

To one professor she wrote the following:

This is just to let you know how grateful I am for allowing me to see you in action. It is your aggressive, rhetorical, daily obsession with yourself that makes

you such a well-known academic racketeer. By observ-
ing you I have come to understand how, by force of
ignorance and self-deception, a man can become a
wretched thing, a wasted thing, a vessel of sorrows.

May your day be fruitful!

This lighthearted patter was the first of many efforts, in which she specialized in being unwelcome. She had a set form of these epistles, for soul-stunted males, which ran:

O blubbery thing! Strip the fat from your soul
before you suffocate! When will you find the supple-
ness, the ease, the lithe surety of a lover! And thank
you for your preening, self-satisfied thuggery, which
has inspired me to seek a life of my own.

I hope, when I am changed, to find you—changed.

Anisetta also liked to write to dead people, like Immanuel Kant:

Immanuel! I like it! Especially that phenomenon/
noumenon stuff. Let's head for those noumena, guy!
No prob! You've got the words; I've got the music.
Let's dance!

And to Sigmund Freud:

Siggie! Thanks for being such a snazzy guy! Too
bad about the clit envy!

But most of all, she wrote her thank-you notes to the powers of this earth, like angels, coyotes, hummingbirds; or to the more abstract eminences, like Reason, or Jokes.

For example, she wrote:

Dear Reason, zany thing that you are,

I'm glad you're around. Some days I'm in love with you, with your panoplies of order, your way of bringing ratio, proportion, exactitude, standards: your way of making sense. When we meditate on something, when we understand how the elements of the world come into necessary, elegant, logical concord, it is a light-making moment.

On the other hand, you should stop being such a cocky brute, striding about and claiming all the world, the whole world, as your own. Who do you think you are, anyway? You are not the only useful thing on this earth: think, for example, of the common pig.

Get the message?

And by these expedients, she soared. And, soaring, she was brought by a course of nature into conclusions about the strange, wild, permanent entitlement of our lives.

As for me, I could not help but want to know what the whole range of these conclusions was. I know only that she thought her notes were more than a metaphysical joke: she thought she knew at least one of the marks that make a life—the manner of its thankfulness.

The last I heard from her was this note:

Dear Dominico,

Thank you for showing me the advantages of skylights in household architecture. There in the light, during all our lunchtime study hours, we have had one of the securities of love: the way we knew as we walked through cool morning air that we could trust a weather that was in us, such a sweetness—

I'm leaving tonight, forever. It's not that I don't love you; it's just that our two souls have made something different of this one love. To me, you are a home I must leave, to make the world my own.

To you, I'm the story you'll never forget.

In the dark
Where you undress
A blooming iris.

—NOBUKO KATSURA

Your spirit, do I not know how to please it?
Bridegroom, sleep in our house till dawn.
Your heart, do I not know how to warm it?
Lion, sleep in our house until dawn.

—A PRIESTESS, CIRCA 2000 B.C.

Unself yourself.

—HAKIM SANAI (12TH C)

For I am the first and the last.
I am the honored and the scorned one.
I am the whore and the holy one.
I am the wife and the virgin.
I am the mother and the daughter.

—FROM "THUNDER: PERFECT MIND," A POEM
BY A WOMAN LIVING IN THE 3RD–5TH C

PART III

*Heard in upper New York State from a woman whom
I visited seeking help in understanding the plight of a
brilliant friend who had been judged insane. He thought
he could hear colors. I had given him Rimbaud to read,
and some weeks later when I visited him he winked at me.
And when I told him this timely story, he looked at me
and said, "For the love of heaven tell that woman that she
must safeguard what she knows. Most of the world will
deny it. From abominable darkness, they will deny it."*

....

WHERE IN THE WORLD IS YOUR WORLD

Our friend Suzanne belonged to the other world, the one that we have all heard about: a trustworthy, forthright, gift-giving world within and beyond our daily affairs. In that place, and only there, she lived knowledgeably, irresistibly. However, Suzanne like the rest of us had to find how she might combine such a world with the momentary world of our practical affairs. In fact, her main task in life was figuring how this integration might occur. To meditate upon such solutions, she took on the habit of walking, and talking aloud, in the forested mountains near her home.

Mountains, she knew, kept secrets.

She wished often that the practical world, all the thresh and smolder of daily events, had more to do with the world where she really lived. Sometimes, when by virtue of her honest, needful concentration she would be touched by the energetic reality of the day; or when her work, reading manuscripts at a small publishing house, would align itself with the most delicious influences of the hour, she would feel the very seasons revolve through commonplace phrases. Sometimes when walking in the country she felt so at home, it was as if sparrows could nest in her thoughts.

When such things happened, she conceived that there might be one day, as it were, a marriage of two worlds, the practical and the real. It would be a marriage that made life whole.

Unfortunately, such unions were rare, for Suzanne's time was taken up by the usual considerations, which settled themselves around her like dry branches, slowly burning her to death at the stake of her arrangements. But she was a strong woman. She kept walking in her beloved mountains; she kept working and searching.

One cold winter day she was sitting with coffee by her window in the morning and she heard the sounds, faint at first, very faint; but she composed herself by means of the coffee and her magisterial heart. She concentrated as the sounds became more distinct. They were very soft, soft as the sound of white mist coming out of an old bottle, before the genie appears.

She stayed by the window for hours, guessing at the source of such a visitation; then she saw the eagle. Deep in her mountains, in a big pine at the high end of a long canyon, an eagle was ruffling his feathers, lifting them and then all at once releasing them back into place. The sound she heard was this gentle extension and settling-back of countless golden feathers.

The sound, all the rest of the hour, of the beautiful eagle, carried her deep into the ordinary day; and so, slowly, all that day, the world unbound her mind and her moments with sound. Later she heard the rushing of clear air over the wings of the eagle when it glided down the canyon.

The whole day changed from within: she would hear something, then have to identify what she heard. She understood that there was a capacity, a special knack of listening; more than attendance to the practice of the world, but a conscious illumination, the making of a place, a time, by movement of understanding—all so that she could know more of what was always present.

The world referred to her in sound. She heard the intricate percussion of myriad sand grains, carried by waves, as they fell roaring on the beaches of a coast she once had loved. She could hear from distant cities the pulse of children not yet one year old, whose hearts were not yet complicated by failure. She could hear grass grow. She could hear the supple give and resistance of bones in the hand of her neighbor at hard work. She could hear the clouds change color, the silken uproar of underground rivers, the ripening of coffee berries on unknown slopes of mountains in faraway tropical forests. She could hear the musical aging of an old wood house, and the acceleration of sap in the roots of big trees during the clap of thunder. She could hear the coarseness of a lie in someone's voice.

And what of the practical world? She saw that the practice of life is just that—practice, and that if we look and listen and work on earth, we might get good at it, quit screwing around, step lively, look askance, find our faces, uncover the midmost of our hopes, take the butcher paper off our hearts—and earn the marvels of a world made permanent.

As we should. For has it not been said, now and again, by women and children and some few others, that our lives are not separate from the world? Our lives are not separate—we are.

Told to me near of the top of the island, much loved by Saint Francis, that is in the center of Lago Trasimeno, in Umbria, a region in the center of Italy. This is a site with a primitive church, where the shadows seem to be at play— almost as if they had heard the Canticle of the Sun.

The storyteller was a former nun married to a former priest. They were both there that day. They seemed aglow.

....

WORK MAY BE GOOD FOR SOMETHING

Once there was a painter who lived in Umbria. She painted rivers, country roads, stone houses; flowers, bridges, fields. This world, she thought in her simple way, was what we see, and more than what we see; what is apparent, and the animate beauty within.

Years passed, and more years, and the painter became famous, quite beyond her intentions, even beyond her awareness. In the land where she worked, and in countries across the oceans, her work was much in demand, and it sold for remarkable sums. Yet this prosperity meant very little in the daily life of the painter. As she had always, she rose early in the morning and began her beloved work.

One day after receiving an impressive check in the mail from the sale of a single piece of hers, she started to wonder if some of the buyers paid not so much for the work itself, but for her very name; so that her paintings risked being merely exhibited, rather than being a source of life. And so, one splendid night over a bottle of Sagrantino, she resolved to begin selling her paintings with more craft and anonymity, with a more impish strategy. Her idea was to have them bought by those who saw value in them, beyond the vagaries of reputation and the movements of the marketplace.

Sometimes she placed her work in galleries under a different name. Sometimes she would sell pieces herself but claim that they were the work of other artists from other countries, or, depending on the style, from another century. Most fun of all, on the days of the big flea market she would gather some household goods and some paintings, and from a booth in the market sell her work for modest offerings to those she saw were examining her canvasses with high-hearted patience and penetrating bemusement. One advantage to such a buyer, of course, was that one day she would discover that the painting on the wall of her little house was worth a treasure fit for a pasha.

All of this felt inevitable, and so our painter began to wonder how she might extend her mischievous activity. And slowly, as day after day she worked, her meditations concentrated within her, and all manner of ideas and stratagems occurred to her. If she, as a guest in someone's house or apartment, saw there an order of beauty in formation, she would wait her chance. Then one day she would return when she knew the house was empty, make her way inside, and hang upon a wall just the painting that would perfect and complete the spiritous reality of the place. Other times she would hear about someone under siege, whether friend or stranger, whether celebrated, obscure, or reviled—and if, by intuition, she thought a certain work of hers would bring some solace or necessary exultation or vision of a safe way forward, she would ship them that very painting from an address that didn't exist.

Occasionally she still would sell a painting under her own name. Since she was distributing most of her work so eccentrically, her identifiable pieces had become much more rare, and so fetched magnificent prices. And no one of the hundreds of people that found money in their house, or in their mailbox, or deposited in their account, was ever able to trace the funds to the painter, who, hard at work, herself forgot how she distributed her wealth.

One day she was at work on a still life—a table covered with a white cloth, bearing a wooden bowl full of peaches, a bottle of red wine, a vase of flowers. As she worked, a peace grew in her, and her brushstrokes were swift and wholehearted, and what took form before her had a power beyond anything she had ever done. For hours she painted, until she was exhausted. She ate a brief dinner and dropped into a deep sleep.

The next morning, full of eagerness, she went to her studio, wanting to give a few final touches to her new creation. Striding to her easel, she saw—a blank canvas. Stunned, she stood rooted and silent. Where was her painting? In desperation she looked around the room, moving aside other canvasses, opening closets, finally roaming through the house. Her still life was nowhere to be found. Had it been stolen? Impossible! What was she to do?

She stood for a long time in her studio. Then, wanting to recapture the transcendent energies of the previous morning, she began again to paint—this time moonlight on a river that ran under a bridge at the border of her home province. And once more the sense of sharp, remarkable peace possessed her, and her brush moved over the canvas with concision and hope and surety. Once more the hours passed, and, exhausted again but full of joy, she went off to a dark and restorative sleep.

Once more, of course, the next morning, upon her easel stood a blank canvas.

She stood a long time, knowing a search would be useless. And then upon the blank canvas she began again to paint, this time an entirely different scene, and her body filled with peace as a jar fills with honey.

The next morning, confronting yet another blank canvas, she set to work again. And so it was for days on end.

One evening she was invited to a dinner in Rome, and with her friends in the Eternal City she joked and told stories and proposed toasts. After dinner a stranger stopped by their table. He looked vaguely familiar, being known, and then only slightly, to one of their company. The stranger invited them all home for an after-dinner grappa. It was not until our painter had settled into a soft chair in the comfortable home of their host, not until she had sipped her grappa and had a chance to look around, that she noticed the side table. It was small, covered with a white cloth. Upon it was a wooden bowl full of peaches, a bottle of red wine, a vase of flowers.

It was exactly as she had painted it—the arrangement on the table, the label on the wine, the color of the flowers, the texture of the cloth, the slanting of the light—exactly.

The shock of it seized her. She could say nothing. Not much later her friends, thinking her tired, took her off to her rooms.

THE NEXT NIGHT, as she passed from Tuscany into Umbria, she could not help but notice the moonlight under the bridge.

Later, back in her studio in her stone house in a small village, she stood before the blank canvas, bewildered. To what work was she called?

And a voice from Beyond said: "Did you think that Creation was once and forever and final? It is not. A part of Creation is renewed every day, and depends upon the hidden ones, the necessary ones, the messengers.

"You are called now to such labor. With your brush, you must paint the world into place. You must do the work that turns into the world."

SHE STOOD QUIETLY for a long time. Then, knowing she was going to work all night, slowly she took in hand a fine brush she had never used. She found on her palette, as she knew she would, the deep gold she needed. She stepped to her canvas, and in thanks, savoring every fateful stroke and radiant line, she began to paint the movement of morning light over the soft and blessed countryside of Italy.

I was in love over twenty-five years ago with a brilliant, daring woman who, wisely, left me. And so I was delighted to come across her many years later at a flea market in Oakland, California, where she sold used books, specializing in haiku, cookery, and painting—especially Persian miniatures.

She told me this story almost as soon as I saw her. It was her way of catching up. She refused to say anything more.

....

THE CASTLE IN THE AIR

Once there was a rebellious woman. She found that it was delightful to challenge the social conventions of her day, and she took an impish pleasure in doing so. Convention, she saw, is largely a matter of expectation; and so when people expected to engage her in, say, a tender and grave exchange of confidences, it was just then she felt herself at her most rowdy and acerbic. When gritty, seething tension was called for, she put on an air of saucy lethargy. When indolence was mandated, she was piping with energy. When at a banquet, and expected to be decorous, she was a roustabout and a maniacal joker. More than once she managed to have herself thrown out of solemn, distinguished gatherings for her ebullient skepticism.

She couldn't help herself: there was nothing more ridiculous than large groups of people submitting helplessly to imprisonment within a cellblock of expectation.

We have all heard of impregnable old castles, with their battlements, their crenels and machicolations; but these walls were nothing compared to the invisible walls of social habits and psychological formulae. In the old days, a soldier might pour down a vat of boiling pitch upon the heads of assailants. These days, we have a still-more extraordinary situation: for society is like a walled city with its battlements turned inward, preventing anyone from emerging. Every time our friend tried, her own companions poured upon her a boiling pitch of assumptions, socially endorsed ignominies, and senseless obligations. Most amusing of all, many went through passionate motions of escape, and by this means attracted attention that fixed them all the more firmly within the walls of their culture.

As well we might expect, our friend had a rowdy, subtle solution to this imprisonment. She decided to build a castle of her own. She meant it to be the castle where she could retreat, whenever she was possessed by the solitary genie of her own reflections. And there was an additional and precious benefit: she now had a place where she could invite the people of her choice—those who were willing to play by the rules of learning, improvisation, experiment, good will, and exactitude.

The only problem was location. Easily solved: she would build her castle in exactly that spot named by one and all as the most foolish and irresponsible: she would build her castle in the air.

And a magnificent castle it was, a dwelling place

for her most private ideas, her long-constructed hopes, her iridescence of mood, her overwrought variety of demeanor, her jokes that fell like spindrift upon the events of the day. It was a castle with arches and gables, with courtyards and open plains, with rooms of cardboard and rooms of marble. It had rooms full of books, and rooms full of tricks. Some of the books were so full of affection that when they were read they gave the reader the sensation of receiving amorous overtures. In the courtyards of the castle there were jugglers who demonstrated the way it was possible for a woman to keep all her dreams aloft, spinning, headed back always into her hands.

And best of all: as everyone was looking toward this castle afloat above the fortified world where we all live, our friend was able to approach unnoticed the big gates of society. As everyone found a way to visit the world she had made for herself, as they entered and mused, marveled and understood, it became the world she had made for everyone else. As the visitors came to know the books and tricks, the songs and dreams of her castle in the air, she came to know an unprecedented peace. Until at last, down in the walled city of society, her moment come, she slipped out the gates and was gone.

There are those who seek valiant adventures to far reaches of the earth. Yet as any parent will know, simply to conceive and raise a child is the most daring enterprise imaginable. Light streams from an infant, and you understand at once how much will be called from you.

These events occurred in the Kings Mountain region, along the California coast. They were related to me, quietly, by the father of the young girl in the story. It is clear she is making him into what he did not imagine he might be. I convey his account, of course, because his small daughter does not have the time to tell her story herself. She has more important work in hand.

....

THE ASTROPHYSICS
OF CHILDREN

I sometimes have a quickening insomnia, and so I rise to read, or to walk around and try to order the gust of words in my head. It takes me hours sometimes; for it is as if I am blown, like a kite, into far regions of the sky where I have only my hope that the string will hold.

Perhaps because of these odd states of mind, I was not surprised by the gleam I saw coming from beneath the door of my little daughter. I was walking the halls of our house around four in the morning, and there it was, a line of light. Still, it made no obvious sense. She was six years old and had just started first grade. She was so tired at the end of the day it was as if she were carrying a sack of rocks to bed. I had thought that she was tired from school.

I swung open her door and saw her standing by the side of her low table. On the table were three spinning cones of light, lovely, effervescent, irresistible. My daughter was studying them, touching them, shaping them. I stood and watched her, not wanting to interfere. In fact, I wanted to leave, feeling like an intruder in my own child's room. Then, slowly, she turned and looked at me with her big green eyes. Then she said:

"Zephyrs!"

And I understood all at once. It was a word she had learned recently, used in high desert country where we hike to refer to the whirlwinds of dust that rise from the sand and stones to turn gracefully across the countryside. I suddenly remembered that on the last trip to the desert with my daughter, we had seen seven zephyrs, which was most unusual. They delighted her; by my side, she had been aglow.

At the door of her room, I whispered to her:

"Show me what you are doing—"

There was a long silence. I could hear only the purring of the little zephyrs. It was playful; new, somehow.

"Daddy, goodnight!" she said happily, and I stepped back and closed her door.

The next morning she was uncommonly affectionate. As I took her to school, she had, as usual, her "project box," which held (we had always been told) her special creations to show her teacher. I could, however, hear the whirring. When I dropped her off, she even winked at me, the little gremlin.

The next time I saw her at work was in the bathtub, in the morning, on a Saturday. For some time she had wanted to bathe herself, which she did happily and at length. After a spell she invited her mother to get in the bath with her, which the two of them loved. Passing by the bathroom, I heard again the same whirring, but this time with a moist, lush savor. I knocked, of course, and she cried out happily:

"Mommy and I have been expecting you! We are ready!"

She had three waterspouts, tiny but distinct, spinning and glistening in the bathtub with her. I remembered that we had promised her that day a trip on a sailboat, out along the shoreline, to visit some coves and bays, have a picnic, watch for whales, whistle for the dolphins. When we left for the harbor later that morning, she took her project box.

By chance, I read the next day in the newspaper about the astonishing waterspouts sighted offshore. There was even a photo taken by an alarmed fisherman, showing three stratospheric, glittering whirlwinds of water moving across the ocean, as if by divine commandment.

She showed me the next project. We live near an open meadow, bordered by a forest of madrone, oak, and redwood. There is a sandy area hidden in a hollow, and she led me there by the hand one Sunday afternoon, to where she had overturned a wooden crate. She lifted it to show me two pairs of small golden stones, each pair set at the head of a compact, closely arranged form made with sinuous lines of bark and leaves. The two forms had a strangely familiar symmetry. And I knew that my insomnia that night would lead me outdoors into the clear night. I confess to a roaring of heart, when I heard two great horned owls calling to each other from low branches in the tanbark oaks.

Her next project needed two years. She had some friends, two other little girls and one lucky boy. They had been playing in the forest every weekend. They told us they had a fort. I glimpsed it from afar, though I knew not to approach until invited.

Each of the four children finally did ask their parents for a picnic, and even now I laugh at the innocence of our acceptance. They had built a shed in the forest, so as to pursue their labors in privacy. Inside they showed us the finished work, set out on the ground. We examined the brilliant arcs in floral beauty around a bright core. They had made it of stones, feathers, paper; in parts it was painted with incendiary colors; in parts it had a sense of tranquil passage, in others a sense of imminent and beautiful catastrophe; in others I heard a kind of atomic hum, as if from a hive of inconceivable powers.

Of course I had promised her a telescope, and that night, taking turns, we found, in deep space, the turning pinwheel galaxy: perfect, boundless, titanic, inevitable. When the children weren't gazing at it, they were holding hands.

Afterward, we all went inside to have some hot chocolate.

I tell you all this so that you will have a record of the most obvious and ordinary things that happen to a parent. That is to say, how the life our children have to make may come to make the life we have, to open the gates of our senses, to answer an ancient longing, to unify mind, earth, and sky.

I have spoken with my daughter, in hopes of finding out how I might qualify myself to learn what I might do with the time I have left.

Language, as everyone knows, has sacred origins. To connect with those origins, we must figure out what we mean when we say the simplest thing. This is a story, I am instructed, "told by a woman for other women." I heard it, privately and unexpectedly, in the New York Public Library. Since that day, it has never been the same, really not at all, to sit down and take up a pen and write any word.

....

WHAT WE MEAN BY BREAD; AND BY SACRAMENT

These days, people want language to render some yield directly, as though language were a kind of money; as though, in writing and talking, we invest in the world. And it is true that in some ways language is like money; except that when you pay for bread, you get just a loaf; but when you *say* bread, you get more than a loaf. You get noon light on the wheat fields, the quickness of foxes wandering in the adjoining forest, the hope for the harvest, the history of stories in the hands of the baker; you get all that bread's venerable associations with heaven, any one of a thousand celebrations at table; you get a living thing that, right there in front of you, may come into amorous concord with the wine and cheese.

Then there is the bakery, with its industry, gossip, moving community, and savory panoramas—all of which is absorbed by the bread you buy. The salt in the bread brings to the loaf the catastrophes of the sea; the butter bears the sweet milk of early morning.

And then, as you bought the bread, there was the man kneading dough under the skylight in the big back room, his forearms covered with flour and his hair disheveled with the joy you have given him each day as you, with your speculative ebullience, stepped into the bakery. He has hazel eyes; he stops to look at you, his hands still in the dough. You realize that the loaf would be decidedly improved in taste if it were not eaten until after you had, in your circumspect way, figured out whether you might rough up this young man in bed.

This culinary speculation, you make known to him. You meet him after work and go home together with old-fashioned grins. He smells like yeast, cinnamon, wheat flour, melted sweet butter. He is shy.

You wonder what he has learned at work.

You find out: afterward you feel kneaded, hot, fragrant, risen, delectable.

So have you made your investment in life and language, you have set forth on your venturing. And although you have your privacy, nonetheless, you and your lover have changed, for all time, one word. The warm afternoon light, the worlds you both brought, the pathways found in one another's hands; the hot generosity and courage of the two of you, the way your heat savored of allspice, the shared thankfulness; the sense of timing and readiness, the deliverance, the lifetime of teasing and durable joy that began on that day: all now is part of what will be meant always, always, everywhere in the world, each moment in the world, whenever someone says—bread.

Told to me one lazy summer afternoon, when I stopped into a bank in London to talk about online management of certain accounts. My banker has an acrobatic wit, bright azure eyes, and a pierced nose. She was once fired because of the piercing, but then rehired immediately because the bank could not function without her.

....

THE BANK OF DAYS

Most people are familiar with the banks of finance, which accept deposits, pay interest, and make loans. The money deposited in these banks represents the value assigned to certain limited human efforts, and everyone agrees that this money can be exchanged for goods and services.

It is useful to examine this common phrase—"goods and services"—for it assumes that anything which can be bought by humankind is either good to have or of service to us. By now we have all learned that this is absurdly, and sometimes tragically, far from the truth. And because of this, a new sort of bank has been created: a bank of days.

This new bank does not accept deposits of money, but only of people's days. When someone has lived a day they think especially amusing, instructive, tasty, or beautiful, they may go to this bank and deposit this day into the common account; for there are no individual accounts at this bank. This is because, as everyone knows, days are not the property of anyone, but belong to the commonwealth of our experience. And so all the deposits in the bank are placed in an account that is held in the name of everyone. The bookkeeping is thus greatly simplified.

Now, this bank cannot, obviously, make loans of money. It does, however, as you may yourself know, loan its days to those judged to be creditworthy, because they may have a legitimate use for amusement, instruction, tastiness, or beauty. The bank has found that the best way to make such loans is not to inform the recipient that she has been loaned a day, but simply to do so, in accordance with management's policies of selection. The expectation is that the interest of the borrower will be sufficient to compensate the bank for its trouble. Let's say, for example, that a depositor trusted by the officers of the bank recommends a certain woman for a loan. If all goes well—that is, if the right day is on deposit and the woman can be found—then the whole range of possible experience held within a remarkable day will be loaned her. The value of this day will be increased by the goods the borrower can discover in it and the services she can obtain.

She might, for example, be loaned a day that has in it the sightings of many falcons, who fall out of the sky with a sure, able, lovely swiftness and silence. Because of these sightings, she might discover in this day the value of falcons as a model for the movement of her thoughts, which must, after patient reflection and vigilance, seize gracefully upon the life-giving conclusion. If she is very successful, she might be provoked to some unrelated offbeat discovery; say, that the falcon's gliding high and still, wings spread, facing into the wind, is meant to teach her how to situate herself, to teach a way of consideration, of reflection, a habit of steadiness—so that she learns, once and for all, how to keep the whole in view. If she learns in just this way, she will, as a matter of course, find the bank and pay back the loan of the day, which, because of the detail of life found in it by the debtor, has increased in value. And, in its changed form, this enriched day can then be loaned to someone else. And before long the day has changed entirely and the bank is considerably enriched.

This is the way the world works. This woman is a real woman. We cannot exaggerate how much we owe her. And how much we owe all the clients of the bank, if in fact they make their faithful repayments.

Such are the wonders of compound interest.

Now, if the woman had found nothing in the day (perhaps she would not even notice the falcons), then the bank receives nothing. This happens now and then because, just as not all loans are repaid, not everyone knows, as they live their days, what on earth to do. Not everyone knows how, in the soil of their hope, there might already be seeds.

So it is that the bank of days takes in deposits and extends its strange loans. You may wonder whether the bank is prospering during these times of ours. But such a question is difficult to answer, because the assets of the bank of days are difficult to measure. We might do well, though, to determine whether our best days are saved in a prudent and responsible way, and whether or not, by our repayment of attention to the splendors we are given, the bank of days will be solvent in the fateful years ahead.

Heard in Kansas in a Laundromat. The teller held forth calmly, though she was pillaged with grief. This story turned me into a student of shadows.

And it confirmed what a number of the other women in these adventures have held to be true: that light has an intelligence of its own, and that it is full of judgments, suggestions, and messages.

....

ONE LITTLE RECORD OF ONE LITTLE DEATH

I tried to warn him. But, as usual, he wouldn't believe me. So let me give you a brief account of the exchange and its aftermath—do with it what you will.

He was my brother, and like everyone, he had a shadow. The sunlight, as everyone knows, creates shadows. It is less frequently noticed that the sunlight, which has its own intelligence, is examining us, and inscribing upon the earth what it sees in us. As a result, our shadows contain a cumulative record of our lives. Over time, each shadow takes on a life of its own. In a good life, it brightens; otherwise, it darkens with violent sorrow.

Which leads naturally to my brother, and to the question of his death. I saw his death coming on, and I thought he should do something about it. As our shadows are brightened, so our lives are extended; until finally, if we live so that our shadows disappear, we may be extended infinitely. I tried to show my brother how this might happen, how he might have the chance to find his way to such radiance. And I told him that his heedless and thrilling life held a risk and a terror, because our shadows can darken, take form, and turn upon us.

But he did nothing, except go on over many years seeking excitement, the admiration and approval of other men, and a daring variety of entertainment. And one day, I saw how his shadow had detached itself slightly from his body. I pointed it out to him, the little sliver of light between his foot and the shadow of his foot. It shook him, and he began to dread the morning light. Sure enough, every morning there was more light between his shadow and him. And then all at once his shadow was completely detached. It was seething, crimson, repulsive.

His shadow stood up beside him, unstoppable. He could see all of himself. The juvenile thrills, the willful ignorance, his daily indifference, the neglect of his chance to cherish, the idolatry of himself, the farce of his loving . . . he saw it all, and much more.

The shadow took hold of the hand inside his hand.

People do not like the look of corpses. But the corpse he left behind looked so beautiful, really so beautiful, compared with the man the shadow led away. That man, my young brother, now was covered with what looked like pus on fire.

Nothing is stranger, nothing, than one certain idea of men. They think that because women forgive them, they will always and forever be forgiven, even by the light of the world.

*I once worked in a bar in Battle Mountain, Nevada,
which is, blessedly, not near anyplace else. I remember the
time fondly because it was in those days I began writing
one sonnet every morning, and four on Saturdays.
I shared this with no one except this woman, an eccentric
house-painter who was so slow in her work, you would
have thought she was in a museum copying an Old
Master. This woman never drank alcohol, except on holi-
days, and then she drank whiskey. One New Year's Day,
she told me this story.*

....

ANGEL-PAINTER

Once there was a woman who was an angel-painter. She
had bolted onto the stone wall at the entrance to her
shop an old brass plaque, which said just that: ANGEL-
PAINTER. At the time she began in her trade, most of the
people in her community had consciously developed
their angelic faculties; and so were they, some of them,
couriers of sunlight, compatriots of moonlight, sidekicks
of rivers, translators of the many-leaved books of the big
oaks. That is to say, their angelic natures were developed;
and though they seemed normal, they had a wide range
of responsibilities in the world. Just like everyone, they
did the work they were qualified for.

It was necessary to paint these angels now and then because of the arduous work involved in that winged profession. Sometimes they would come to her as a group, dirty and bedraggled, windswept and fatigued by their trips all over the earth in search of a nondescript flower whose petals, infused in water from a spring hidden in mountains, would make a potion to cure a little girl who was deathly sick. They did this, of course, because this girl, as a woman, would by her gentleness and learning save a whole country from destruction.

But more often they would come singly: one angel, who lived many of his years as part of the ocean, had been given the task to fall at the right moment as enormous storm waves, just as a certain young woman walked by herself on the beach. The waves rocked her with such joys that in later years she was able to put all the seven seas into one sonnet. When the ocean-angel, preparing for such work, had come to our painter, she had restored to him the glossy rhythms and prophetic gatherings of salt water; so, later, along a wild shoreline, there was just the concentration of beauty meant for someone who did not know she was meant to write verses.

Other angels would come to her: those who had just worked all night long to plant cottonwood seeds in a high desert canyon. This work they did so that years later in a spring grove of big trees a doe could find shelter she desperately needed; all in order that the first steps of the fawn born there would by seen by a priest who had sought the wilderness in hopes of healing his mad heart. And so it was that by the example of the fawn, the priest was able to give to the phrases of his next sermon a motion that held the beginning of grace.

Yet another angel, painted, in a bit of fun, to look just like a human, wore himself out standing in the hot sun all day selling books that were alive: if these books were opened, they would, then and there, attend closely to the thoughts of the one who held them, and the book upon its pages would set forth exact and uncanny stories that included the most intimate details and propositions about the reader. It was a perfect ruse, since it was important to take people by surprise, and most people think that they read books, but not that they may be read by a book.

To those who did the more classical work of angels, and so did not need to alter their traditional form, our painter gave fresh coats to brilliant robes, she touched up radiance of a halo, she sharpened the line and set of a wing. For those more outrageously inclined, who might be called upon to become anything or anyone in the world, her work was arduous and various: with her magic strokes she painted the receptive angel's form in accord with any worldly necessity—she might become a gazelle, a redwood, a waterfall—whatever was apposite to the task at hand.

As hard at work as she was, it was lucky that, later on, the angel-painter noticed when the more conventional people in the area increased in numbers. A few of her clients were jailed, or even put to death for not having a useful vocation that everyone could understand. An angel who ran as a clear spring creek was injured when the creek was dammed and turned to a stagnant pool. A gathering of angels standing as aspen trees in the autumn on a hillside, showing all their gold, was razed to the ground by a chain dragged between two tractors.

A winged angel was stripped bare, and her feathers used to decorate hats. What formerly was known to be divine was now by a terrible distortion of history taken to be merely supernatural, fabricated, or useless.

Under these conditions, thought our painter, how could the angelic work go on? With angels imperiled, who would tend to the hidden work that holds together our world? Alarmed as they were, the angel-painter and her luminous clients came up with a plan: whatever the labor, in whatever form necessary, to be undertaken in the world, our worker would, when they returned to her, paint *all* the angels to look like humans. They could always, as the centuries moved through them, come to her at a later date for their change into the form of life needed—the star, the flower, the phrase, the hope, the miracle. But once the task was done, they had to be repainted; each of them had to be disguised again, to hide away their mischief, their hopefulness, their radiance. And our angel-painter, she would focus her skills, she would specialize in giving back to these boisterous spirits a human form and color, so that the community of divine assistants could not be so easily attacked. She would paint them to look just like everyone else.

And so she did.

To this day she continues her work, renewing the human look of those she loves. Of course, since there are not many angel-painters, she cannot always set to work when she is needed. And so you may notice a wing becoming visible on the back of your neighbor, or wildflowers and forest shadows showing through the veins of your postman; you may, when you call the plumber, be startled by a hollow place in his forehead where oceans and stars can be seen.

When this happens, then follow these people, for they will soon be on their way to the angel-painter. And it may be that you too had once felt her thunderous brush but had gone out in the world, and, in the pitch and commotion of daily affairs, forgot your real work.

Told to me by a tough, enterprising Dutch woman who had sailed around the world three times. I met her in a museum in The Hague, where I had gone to see a certain Vermeer. As it turned out, she had gone there to see the very same painting.

Even when she was walking, or speaking, she was sailing. During each of her circumnavigations, she had nearly died. She was planning a fourth.

. . . .

SHE CLAIMS THAT EVEN TIDAL WAVES MEAN SOMETHING

Tidal waves are contained within the ocean and are not visible until their devastating embrace of land. As these waves move through the sea, small sailboats may be lifted gently, as by a long swell, and no one aboard will know that a titan has passed beneath.

It is said that, in a similar way, a reality is contained within the world and moves toward the coastline of our lives. Those who deal in the surface of things notice only a long swell that affects day-to-day events but slightly. But as it passes, those who know the depths will take heed, remember, love, make jokes, labor with light and air, warn, and watch. They are, in other words, just like the rest of us: here, in part, to learn the possibility, the usefulness, and the inevitability, now and then, of devastation.

*It must be said that this storyteller is a woman imperti-
nent about almost everything else, as well. I understood
her to be formed by the history of her country, a mind-
bending mix of life-giving beauty and grisly violence.*

*She is Spanish, very funny, very beautiful, and lives
in Salamanca. She's enough of a reason for any man to
uproot himself and move to Salamanca.*

....

SHE IS IMPERTINENT
ABOUT TRAGEDY

The world is evolving toward perfection.

Consider this: as thieves perfect their boldness
and treachery, and so improve their art, there will come
eventually a thief who will steal thievery from the world.

Even more important: there will come a terrible
band of killers who will murder all the other killers; and
then, as they do always, turn upon each other.

This is not to say that those who want peace can
stand down and do nothing. They must, for instance,
make sure that thievery does not reassert itself in our
world, because of people who think it's risky, daring, sub-
versive, and exciting. It should be pointed out that these
qualities often distinguish activities that are idiotic.

And as to the killers: once they have eliminated one another, we must make sure that we remember their names in a museum of savagery and abomination. It must be a museum that is finely conceived, clean, efficient, and a credit to our community and our admirable public spirit. The rooms will be kept unreasonably hot, so that everyone will want to use the drinking fountain, and find out what human blood tastes like.

*A reflection on evil, this time straight from a doctor who
worked in an insane asylum where I volunteered, near
Stanford University. This particular asylum was for military personnel, and she heard many stories of unspeak-
able violence. One day as we were sitting together in her
office at the end of the shift, she turned loose this bitterly
reasoned outburst.*

*She told me later that she discovered a small group
of patients who once had worked in vaudeville. They all
adored her.*

....

THE GOOD DOCTOR
TURNS LOOSE A
TIRADE ABOUT EVIL

Tension and relaxation, elation and disappointment, tri-
umphs and setbacks, all our internal feelings and the evident sagas of clarity and health, confusion and sickness:
the alternation of these things is supposed to consti-
tute a life. But what if these things are mere derivatives,
hangers-on, mess-makers, intrusive and obnoxious rela-
tives? What if we are supposed to stand forth and leave
behind that yapping crowd? What would we feel?

We'd feel solitary. We'd be obliged, out of the fetid pool of our own conceptions and emotions, to dry out; and, there in the sun, to talk to ourselves, as preparatory to talking with someone else.

MAYBE WE COULD return to tradition. Tradition has it that there are two kinds of ideas and emotions. The first kind are the degenerate artifacts of culture, history, personality, conditioning, assumptions. The second kind are those derived from pure attributes of soul. They resemble one another, as the tempting, luscious grapes on an old vineyard resemble a bottle of vintage, complex, rich, necessary wine.

But why make wine when one could eat, when one could add the grapes to a table sagging with a weight of food, various in its presentation of sweetness and savors? Why not stuff ourselves with the news, bulk up our thoughts with the fat of the times, make ourselves a part of the exciting stories of our age?

There are other advantages: emotional lard does not have the external discomforts of physical obesity. It is curious, though, that such efforts are expended warning people about the dangers of obesity, and treating those who suffer from such overindulgence. Yet very little attention is paid to those who have contracted a much more widespread and virulent malady: those who are enlarded with themselves.

This is in keeping with a strange cultural preference of ours: that we take aggressive measures to eliminate nuisance and to attack melodramatic, hateful, obvious evil; but we are affably incurious about our internal, continuous evil, which makes all the other kinds possible.

So it is that evil in the world has its reign—not by any special capacity or power, but because of the emotional and ideological bond people have with themselves, and so with each other.

It's a social activity, the way people belong first to themselves, then to each other. The society of evil then is our humdrum social club. We kill each other, in classic murder-suicides. We use the most lethal and dependable weapons in the world: our contented approval of ourselves; our passionate plans; heartfelt, laborious opinions; the elation of our thriving and the bitterness of our pain—everything we feel about who we are. So do we defend and define ourselves, as part of an inconsolable striving for assurance that we are in some way real. We crave that reality. Desperate to have it, desperate to be sure, to do something decisive, affecting, irrevocable—we kill, we are killed. It makes all of us count, at last, for something. We glow with accomplishment, with action, with history, with drama. It can take a lifetime. And many honors are bestowed upon us for these efforts, because what is admired nowadays is using death to make a difference. What matters is doing ourselves to death, and winning recognition and approval for it.

Such a plan. Foolproof, almost.

Told to me in northern California near the Lost Coast, which is, along with parts of Big Sur, the last wilderness coastline in the state. It is known for its fog, redwoods, legends, earthquakes, and marijuana. The woman who shared this story with me would not even give me her name. She did give me, however, a small, flat, smooth piece of wood, such as she used in place of canvas, in her work as a painter. The wood had beautifully finished portraits on both sides.

. . . .

THE GRANDMOTHER

Once on a cliff by the sea there lived an old woman, who each year invited her grandson for a summer visit. Living near this old woman was a little girl the age of the grandson; and it was this circumstance that was specially delightful, for the two were boisterous and fantastical playmates, whose endless dreaming antics at seaside left their bodies toughened with salt and their minds overcome with maritime beauties.

At night, the grandson could never by any ruse or childish knavery persuade his beloved friend to accompany him home. So he would go and dine with his grandmother, and after dinner fall exhausted, exalted, delighted into the old woman's arms, then to be carried gently in by the fire where he would sit, warm and cherished, and listen to stories of the sea.

Now the grandmother, an old sailor of ocean-crossing schooners, had many a tale: about the time in the South Pacific when during a tempest a storm-petrel with an injured wing had fallen upon the deck, and how her crew nursed the bird back to health and learned from her a subtle cry that calms the troubled seas; about shape-shifting dragons who were sometimes big as islands and sometimes small as men's eyes; about the sylphs and ocean-witches, women who walk along the tops of waves and carry cyclones in the tips of their fingers; about sailors bewitched by sharks, who thereafter roam the world in terrible hunger, eating only the souls of other men; about dolphins that burst from the sea and land in the crow's nest of ships, there to leave a blessing of playfulness before they arc back into the water. And it was in part because of these nighttime stories and the sailing, salt-white, wing-wide hours with the girl who romped with him through the daylight, that the young boy grew into a gentleman of blessed and peaceful abilities; and his surety of conscience and breadth of heart were uncommon on this earth.

Our gentleman was still a young man when death took his grandmother out of the warm house. And he was in the middle of his years on earth when he met once again his childhood friend. She had lived an extraordinary life as a painter of landscapes, roaming all over the world. Her paintings were full of irrepressible energies; it was almost as if the sea moved within the landscape of her canvasses. Our friend found her familiar beyond the coincidence of memory and affection.

Finally, when he was himself old, he received from the woman, now also in her old age, an invitation to visit her on the coast where they once had gamboled together as children. He set out immediately, and found his childhood playmate had been changed by the years—into his grandmother.

"How could this be?" he asked.

"I was both your grandmother and a little girl," the old woman said.

"But how?" he asked.

"You were so dear to me that I doubled my life to be able to care for you as a friend during the day and as your grandmother in the evening."

"Such things are possible, then?"

"Such love is possible," his old friend said. "Everyone thinks that immortality would be a good thing. They should take a moment to ponder what they might do with such a gift. Loving you the way I have is what I have done. One of the things I have done."

And so did our gentleman go on his way, to let his mind work upon these secret things. As to the way his new knowledge transfigured him—that is another story.

The old grandmother, alone in her house again, lit the fire and began to prepare certain stories for a grandchild of hers, who was of the age to delight in a visit to the seaside. The invitation had been made, and the child would be arriving that very day.

I was buying postcards in Bend, Oregon, and the woman
behind the counter invited me to coffee. She delighted
me abundantly, not least with this story. The wild open
spaces of the American West hold some of the most
remarkable women in the world: tough, funny, uncom-
promising, brilliant, capable.

....

A COUNTRY GIRL IN
THE CITY CANYONS

Riata, raised in the high desert of the American West,
was stunned when she moved to the city. Though she
liked the hubbub and the irrevocable fevers, the savory
hopefulness and irritable jubilation of city dwellers,
she thought she saw one particular problem: The city
thought it could concentrate the whole world within
itself. All that was beautiful and fascinating could be
incorporated within itself. It discussed itself, worked
according to its own understanding, analyzed the world
by its own rules and suppositions. It looked to the present and the future and took destiny into its hands. The
city thought, in other words, that the world could be
made familiar and human. And, as far as it went, this
was all fine.

There was, though, an important problem: the world is not human. And so in their attempt to live as if the world could be made over in our own image, Riata and her city friends, however much fun they had, were playing out a glittering and useless lie.

Riata knew she had to take action. She returned to her home grounds; she walked through the high desert in the spring when the meadowlarks teased her with raucous suggestions. She visited once more the little bars in her hometown where she waited to drink her whiskey until the transcendent second when it was the warmth of her hand. She went out to see the mustangs come in noon light to the spring just below a limestone outcropping— the roan stallion, four mares, two little foals, circulating slowly there in dusty astonishment and satisfaction.

By these things, she recovered the old, commonplace gifts that in her girlhood had tricked her into hopefulness—gifts that recreated a woman beyond her personal ideas and preferences. But she understood the necessity of this: since the world is not human, the joke is on us—and there's work to do.

This journey having been accomplished, she went back to the city, and studied how she might introduce these necessary visitations from a next world, which is this world. And so she did the obvious thing—she went to the phonebook and, choosing names at random, began writing postcards.

The postcards were usually one-liners, such things as:

> *You are the guardian of starlight, and so you've*
> *got to figure out how to work nights with good grace.*

If you are not funny, it's a lot harder to inherit
the earth; for if you cannot laugh, how are you going
to tell a story about the deadly serious work you are
meant to do?

You want wisdom; but maybe you need pancakes.

If, say, on the sun, you join two atoms together,
you can make light. What would happen if, say, on
earth, you joined two souls?

Total eclipses of the sun are caused by the wink of
a certain tropical songbird; the movements of the sun,
moon, and earth are fortunately synchronized.

You are the one, here is the secret, now is the time,
and perhaps you shouldn't be so infernally proud just
because you have the ability to pull off a suicide that
takes seventy-five years.

Angels can cook with your thoughts and taste you
with their smiles. Do you know what to do with them?

On the branch of your years, one day, the flower of
what you say. Unless the frost of your ignorance kills it.

Disguise yourself wildly, madly, improbably; be
the cement truck filled with honey.

Such were the messages received with regularity all
around the city; Riata sent thousands of cards every year.
And to what end, with what effect, by what justification?

These questions are easy to answer, and you might as well do so. Send her a postcard.

She would be delighted. For of those who have received postcards from her, so few, so very few, have replied.

Told to me by a writer in Utah, whom I met in Dark Canyon, along the upper reaches where the sandstone walls arch up and go through the clouds. She is so famous under her pen name that it makes her laugh out loud. I would venture to say she is on a first-name basis with the spirits who course through this enigmatic canyon, every day, and every night.

....

THE BOOKS WERE SO BAD, SHE SET OUT TO MAKE THE WORLD FROM SCRATCH

Since books have become commodities, the culture has gotten lackadaisical. That is, it does not recognize that, by what is now thought to be a contemptible, old-fashioned criterion, a good book is a common, clear, useful gift: a lens focusing the light of our attention upon an irresistible, grace-giving reality beyond words, within this world. Neither, in general, do we any longer recognize that there are a thousand and one chances to find our way, that we need the right form at the right time, that the truth has to do a cartwheel, go wrong, get dirty, whisper to a lover, take a rest, sip a whiskey now and then.

Good books were once so conceived. And bad books, they were said—by one or another curmudgeon—to be a cancer of the understanding. They kill our classical hopes, misconceive our most florescent pleasures, cringe and wallow in bitterness and tragedy, and deny with grim pride the possibility of crafted, lucid, complete lives.

But, we thank our stars, these judgments do not have to be made anymore! Books are not given; they are traded: like pork loins.

It has simplified the task of the writer: all she has to do is go to the recipe book.

The critic, however, has a tougher job: he has to gorge himself on professional dishes and risk dying of a fatty soul.

And where is the reader in all of this? Waiting there, in her blessed, life-saving skepticism, in her expectant understanding, in the concinnity of a future she hopes for, because she can see where we might go. Since she is not wholly pleased by the books thrust upon her, she is going to have to write her own.

It's rumored that she has taken this effort to its logical extension: she is making a language of her own, creating extraordinary words for use in her manuscripts. The other day, a word of hers was found that had flecks of mica in it, so that it glittered in the sun. Another word was seen to have tattoos, as if it had been drinking in bars in big seaports. Yet another, held in the hand, twirled around and did acrobatic stunts.

When will she, with these new words, make sentences? And as to her books, where might we find them, what is she proposing to us?

She is telling stories—they make coyotes howl, provoke geysers out of the ground, lure songbirds out of the sky and into the house, and have, in general, ordinary and easy commerce with the world.

To put it another way, the stories she is telling are not about herself. She no longer looks into the world in hopes of seeing herself. She has set such coarse obsession aside, in favor of the world, the subtle and brazen life within it, the opalescent pattern of events, the slow-dance of night and day.

It is as if soil and wind, light and flower, now have work with her; so, as she writes, can she be the messenger of what she finds, and what she finds is what was always awaiting her.

In other words, as we read, as we live, we are ourselves being read, studied, contemplated. The world which has us in hand, when we take in hand a good book, bears an intelligence which in some historical periods (periods now thought by our culture to be ignorant and irrelevant) has even been given a name: reality. This is one of the reasons why all good readers will thrive, now and forever—they're in the one company, the one and only company, whose hopes for us, attention to us, and need for us, never fail.

And there's another, evermore obvious reason: language and light have the same origin. And so the reader, at last, with surprise, with joy, goes with her book to a place she knows, because there she is swept up in a destined, beckoning, open spectrum. There she can, as she has been meant to always, read and study and answer the decisive signals in ordinary daylight.

She will answer, and we will live.

*Told to me by an old woman, in the village of
Maidenhead, England, not far from London. I have
reason to suspect she was Nancy, such was the delicious
satisfaction she took in the details of this account. I
remember so clearly the music of her English, the mint
green of her eyes, and her teasing way of telling a story,
both courteous and amorous.*

....

PROPOSITION FOR NANCY

Our friend Nancy was accustomed to seeing on the
street all manner of clever beggars, sharpers, bunco men,
catcallers, bankers, and friends. That is, she lived in a city,
and found sustenance in its bellicose, happy-go-lucky,
perilous days. And so it was that while walking about,
she was not startled by the approach of a well-dressed
gentleman who bowed to her and with a homely, winning smile requested her permission to make a "noteworthy, if not supernatural proposition." Now, propositions
were not unknown to our Nancy, who had received
them left and right, day and night, presented smack in
the middle of the morning, tucked in the last corner of
twilight, in plain view of the afternoon sun, in the promising darkness of the night.

Nancy would listen to anyone, to assess his or her inventiveness, if nothing else. And so she listened: the gentleman proposed that he might be allowed to give her various gifts as the day progressed, gifts that were, he implied suavely, essential to her. The only condition was that she not inquire precisely what use would be proven for each of these gifts.

The inquiry being made, her suitor stood patiently for her reply. Nancy gazed at him slowly and critically; she pondered how best to make a circumspect yet hard-boiled decision; she held her thoughts up to the light to study the reflections that they made; she pondered, she cogitated, she hacked and spat.

Finally she said: "Sure, why the hell not? What have you got for me first?"

And the man gave her five hundred dollars cash, said he would be seeing her soon, and vanished. Abrupt fellow, thought Nancy; and she went on with her errands.

Nancy had not counted three blocks when a burly man came from nowhere, seized her, and dragged her into tarnished shadows in the far corner of an alley. Whirling around to see if anyone had observed him, he fell flat on his face. Picking himself up, and looking as sheepish as ever a thief has looked, he drew a pocket-knife, and while trying to open it he cut himself severely. Next, while trying to rip his shirt to make a compress to stem the bleeding, he broke two fingers—

"Are you new at this?" asked Nancy.

"It's my first time," replied the thief timidly.

"Could I offer you five hundred dollars for that knife?" she asked.

"Sold," he said.

He handed her the knife, she gave him the money, and she helped him dress the wounds sufficiently for a trip to the hospital. At the hospital, what with his tom-foolery of injuries, he rendered up (including gratuities) two hundred dollars for the care received. Once on his own, the man marched forthwith to the opticians to buy eyeglasses, for his sight was subject to the most wretched distortions. It was his desperate, honest, soul-deep need for eyeglasses that had driven him to attempt a robbery; and had, by a secret operation of fortune, led him to Nancy. With the glasses he was able to see what he had been about to see when his eyes began to fail; that is, a series of religious visions given him, numerously and freely.

So was he able to study, in the vernacular of light, messages sent to him, lessons meant for him. He saw exactly how a good couplet can make dance music rise out of city streets. He saw the detail of future centuries in the speech of certain children. He saw how the steps we take in our travels, if made with the right combination of fidelity and good laughs, do not trace out the treasure map, but set down in detail the treasure itself. He saw just how to open an idea to let in the correct amount of sunlight. And knowing by the correction of his sight all these things, he began to write up what he had learned. Though his manuscript has not yet been published, it has been circulated privately, and is said to be most highly regarded by readers of little stories.

As to his remaining money, he surrendered it to a man whom he knew was about to do, for lack of money, a desperate, foolish thing; and to another curious fellow who needed extra cash to buy an excellent meal at a coffeehouse, in which place this gentleman would meet Nancy, and there begins—but that is another story . . .

To return to *this* story, Nancy left the hospital and had not sauntered two blocks before she ran into the courtly gentleman whose cash and prophecy had started all this nonsense—

"Well," said Nancy, "what trouble are you going to get me into now?"

"A very surfeit of trouble, I hope, my precious young woman," replied the gentleman.

"Out with it," said Nancy.

In answer the gentleman held out to her a single coin, of small denomination, and bade her take it. She did, with some disparaging remarks on how brief a flourishing has generosity in this world. She was aware, though, that the buying power of a coin did not necessarily represent its value. And so she went on her way, and soon found herself detained on the street by two arguing men, who implored her to settle their differences. They were arguing about heaven and hell, truth and freedom, the merits and disadvantages of industrial development, the hopes and iniquities of art and science; and both were now entangled so thoroughly in the net of point and counterpoint, proposal and rebuttal, that they had decided to ask the first passerby, Nancy, to settle all these outstanding issues by flipping a coin. Such is the history of ideas.

By inspiration, Nancy pulled from her pocket the very coin given her by the gentleman, and as the two adversaries watched, she flipped it high in the air. As it rose, its rate of spin increased until it was so rapid it threw sunlight in all directions and, of course, made the street sparkle with the oracular fire usual to such moments; and so spectacular was the luminous play that no one really noticed that the coin was not descending. And sure enough, from the radiant space high up where the coin had been there suddenly arched long strings of circus-colored confetti that reminded them all of the necessity of celebration. Champagne and cheap beer were brought. A slide guitar and good chamber music were heard. The world was a painting, the jokes were robust, and clowns massed for a charivari. There was seen at the end of arguments a life where the bolts and shackles fall clanking from our thoughts.

The party lasted all night. As for the men who were arguing, they eventually proved how all honest arguments, just like rivers, lead to an ocean we may describe as—but that is another story. Let us find Nancy, who, in the high satisfaction of fatigue, walked the streets again and encountered there her gentleman friend.

"You!" she exclaimed. "That was some trick with the coin."

"A trick, maybe," he said. "But everything has its price."

"What's the charge?" she asked.

"The very same coin," he replied.

And she held her hand out so that the coin, spinning still high up in the air, could find her and fall again into her grasp.

"There you are," she said, handing it back to him. "What do we do now?"

"This time," said the gentleman, "I am going to give you something you are now in a position to appreciate."

"And so?" said Nancy warily.

"I give you this: I give you nothing at all."

"At least we're still at work," she said cheerfully.

"Good day to you, my dear woman," said the gentle-man, "and good-bye."

She watched sadly as he walked away. And, being given nothing, she felt an unusual need to consider her future. She wandered off to a secluded coffeehouse, a favorite place of hers, pervaded by the aroma of espresso and the tranquility of fine old friendships. The only available chair was at the table of a stranger, who beckoned to her. Without hesitation she sat with him. He, of course, was ready to buy her an excellent meal, and they talked about onions and epics, honeysuckle, justice, pleasure; about little fables, whose readers always go on to travel in savory, inconceivable lands; about the man's brother, a maker of supernatural propositions, and about the amorous undertakings the evening promised.

Later, they went off together into the twilit streets. The city was quiet, the air cool; they walked close, and as a long story found life within them, between them, because of them; as the spiritous, artful night, attentive and trusting, came to take them home; as their hands joined and told the truth, the story where they met ended.

This story was sent to me from Argentina, by the sister of a friend of a friend. We had met very briefly, established a common interest in Borges and Neruda (who didn't even like each other), and so decided to write to one another.

Yet this story is the entirety of the only letter I ever had from her. She appended a note that said, "So how many pennies do you have, you fool?"

....

THE PANHANDLER

Once there was a woman who, through strange and random circumstances, lost her job. She took it hard, as might have been expected, for she was down on her luck anyway. Everything seemed to have gone wrong at once. She had wild mood swings, was easily offended, got discouraged, and had terrible feelings of remorse about a failed love affair. She suffered occasionally from sneak attacks of accidie, a general lack of concentration, and an addictive personality. In other words, she was just like the rest of us when bad times make an unholy alliance with a bad mood.

Unlike most of the rest of us, however, she decided to put off getting a new job, and she hit the streets as a beggar. She had never begged for anything in her life, nor even considered it; and so she had the brilliant success of the blessedly ignorant. It may have had something to do with the signs she made, which bore appeals such as:

LOOKING FOR A SPECULATIVE INVESTMENT? TRY ME

CLOSEOUT BEGGAR! ONE WEEK ONLY!
GIVE WHILE YOU CAN!

ALCHEMIST HERE! I CAN MAKE GOLD
OUT OF YOUR SPARE CHANGE

THE SMALLEST GIFT WILL MAKE MY SOUL
STAND UP AND TAPDANCE

I AM A FALLING STAR—MAKE A WISH

By such expedients, she gathered enough money to rent an apartment and get back to work. But things were different: her mind, resuscitated by the sign-making arcana of her begging career, now had a new shape. She resolved to give everything she made away to those who needed it. And she could, somehow, tell who needed it, just by observing them.

So she did the obvious thing: she went back on the street and panhandled—except that instead of looking for people who would give money to her, she looked for people who would accept money from her. At first, people were startled when she walked up to them to ask:

"Would you like some spare change?"

"Would you be averse to accepting a gift from a stranger, whom you will never see again, but who nevertheless wants you to be able to see the truth of the matter at hand?"

"I'm working for food and for you. Take this."

"I am summertime. This is a plum."

And so on. Unfortunately, she was shunned. It turned out to be far easier to beg for money until someone chose to help her, than it was to give away money to recipients she chose herself. Almost no one would accept anything from her. Those who did prospered strangely. And, on the chance that more of those who want a strange chance would come along, she continued her work on the street. One day, a green-eyed, uncompromising, adventurous, quiet, amorous man stopped and listened to her thoughtfully. He took the coins she offered. He was an engineer from Brazil who designed microprocessors and did the samba, and he asked if he might take her home to South America and marry her. She asked if they might do the samba right there in the street and go to dinner together and perhaps tomorrow morning think about marrying. So did their promising conversation begin.

Thus she was led to the strange conclusion that, contrary to what is promulgated as common sense, many of us are not selfish, but have a capacity for generosity. Unfortunately, it is not enough, not nearly enough, to be generous. It is the merest beginning. The next step is far more difficult: the generous must find a way to recognize and accept the good fortune presented to them every day. So many fail to give the gifts they have because they cannot benefit from the gifts they are offered.

Or, as she put it: if you won't accept small change, there's no way you'll be able to afford paradise.

Rainy cottage—
After lovemaking
The scent of jasmine tea.

—IKUYO YOSHIMURA

❧

Heaven doth with us, as we with torches do,
Not light them for themselves.

—SHAKESPEARE

❧

The candle is not there to illuminate itself.

—NAWAB JAN-FISHAN KHAN (19TH C)

❧

Had I not seen the sun
I could have born the shade
But light a newer wilderness
My wilderness has made.

—EMILY DICKINSON

❧

PART IV

I have never known a woman as taciturn as the teller of this story. She is the most watchful, perhaps the most mindful, person I have ever known. She lives on an island in a lake in the Adirondacks and loves Sappho, Boccaccio, and Camus.

....

THE SILENT WOMAN

Once there was a woman who talked a great deal. She felt obliged to do so, because her opinions about herself, her life, and the world needed to be sustained by talk. It was as if her innermost motivations and dearest principles were held in everything she said—in her pitch of voice and selection of words, the accompanying emphasis of hands, the telling changes of her face. No matter how abbreviated the exchange of words, no matter what subject was brought forth, no matter what the overall situation, this woman's talk held everything about her life.

In this, of course, she was just like many men and women.

At a certain point in her years, however, our talker took on another task, the perfection of her silence. She found that her silence, which had always been around, had a range of meaning and subtlety overpowering that of words; and so she sensed new powers, which, if she could develop in herself, would permit her to be of better service to her cohorts.

This project was difficult, however, because just as each word has a sound and significance, and is subject to rules of grammar and usage, so each silence is different from another, has its own properties, and is subject to the rules of an invisible, beautiful grammar—call it an earthly grammar, since our planet uses no words to give forth its flourishing show.

First she noticed that each silence had a particular shape, and was meant to fit, like a puzzle piece, into a given situation. Then, of course, the force of the silence had to be calibrated, because one too powerful for a given conversation could press upon those present and undermine the phrases which they did speak. Next, she learned that each silence had a certain internal color; and so its hue, brightness, and tone had to be arranged to harmonize properly with the events at hand—to take its place, as it were, within the whole painting of the conversation. Our friend worked on all these fronts, so that the shape, force, and color of a given silence would be consistent with the best hopes—even with the unknown hopes—of those in her company.

After a time, she became valued for her capacity to use silence, along with words, to help people to see, in tranquility, the way forward they needed most; or, alternatively, to see themselves for the dear, ridiculous people they really were. Her provision of the most useful silence was not always obvious to those she helped, because they were used to sustaining their world with talk, rather than with the silent understanding that brought to words a necessary enrichment and power.

Our friend, though, no longer looked to talk for sustenance, for she knew that real language was not of words, but used words. And so her own talk was no longer a personal, uncontrollable revelation, but, at last, had come now to be founded upon the more obvious, comprehensive silence—the silence of the movement of earth through space. This is, of course, the model for the movement of love in darkness, and for the movement of meaning through a sentence. All of which will come clear to the reader as soon as this story, learning at last from its own narrative, finds its way to a necessary silence—its own.

The great European city Barcelona has a reputation for
wealth and eccentricity, for beauty and anarchy. It is
a city that is changed, now and then, profoundly and
forever, by the concentrated work of a few people. I heard
this story in a Cuban restaurant near the cathedral of
Santa Maria del Mar, in the neighborhood of La Ribera.

....

A NUN AND HER LOVING

I am the granddaughter of a nun, and so I am able to
tell you part of the secret history of the nineteenth century. You may not believe me. But I am old, and I want
to die with one less secret. The sweep of events, as usually described, is meant to deceive us. The real history
of the world—what really happened—is mostly secret.
Out of sight, beyond the trumpeting and vainglory, the
strutting and disgust, the declarations of tribunals, the
flourished signatures—beyond all this, within all this,
real work is being done.

A few ideas—say, having schools for children, abol-
ishing slavery, making nations, inventing the loom, making art and nature move together, perfecting a soul by
means of beauty—a few ideas, which had been around
for a while, are known to have taken on particular force

in the nineteenth century. My grandmother was a nun in Spain, one of a special group of nuns in many countries (they all knew each other). These powerful women, with their blessings, dinners, private ceremonies, with their social presence and potent quiet influence, had a hand in many of the seemingly random encounters where such ideas and movements took form and had life in the world.

I can tell you how my grandmother played her part. First of all, she could read the souls of men, just by looking at their shadows. It's lucky for her that she lived in a sunny climate, where it's easier to examine shadows. In England, for example, her work would have taken much longer.

She read souls, so as to find from such reading just when someone quickened within, when he was most available to ideas, to hope, to beauty, to reality. And when she noted two men coming at the same time to the incendiary point when life rises within them like fireworks, then she would take action. She would bring such men together at just the moment when their ideas and energies might merge, lighting up decades, or centuries.

I give you merely one example. In 1878 in Barcelona, a businessman and an eccentric young architect were persuaded by her to visit, at the same hour of the day, a workshop in the city. She had spoken to both men privately. Both men had religious inclinations, and they listened always to her courteous and gentle suggestions. In fact, both of them loved her, but that is another story. So it was that, by her ministrations, yet, it would seem, by chance, the two men met on the appointed day, at the workshop.

The businessman was of astounding wealth. The young architect had almost no experience. He had designed some streetlamps that were never built; a florist stand and a urinal, also never built. His only completed projects were a display case for gloves and his own work desk. He had also designed his personal business card, even though he had no business.

The two men began a friendship that lasted nearly forty years. The businessman is Eusebi Güell, and the architect is Antoni Gaudí. Because of that meeting, they made buildings together that blessed and inspirited the history of Barcelona, and the history of Europe. They made a new marriage between the beauty of nature and the beauty we make as men and women. They showed us how playfulness may be sacred. They changed the way beauty may come forth among us; and now we cannot imagine the world without them.

I have all my grandmother's letters from the two men. So I do not have to guess at the playfulness of their loving. Or at the way some paradise that is here with us played with them.

None of it would have happened without her. Think of her and her friends, in their international amusements, over so many centuries, with such anonymity. Do you think we would have a world left, without them? Even the shred of a world, without them?

In central Nevada there are still groups who go out to hunt big cats, with unpredictable results. I did not know, however, that they were quite this unpredictable. I heard the story in a bar, of course, in Ely, Nevada. Just to the east of this town there stands the 12,000-foot Mount Moriah, which has a long flat top called The Table, near where these hunters sought their prey, and their prey, them.

....

THE HUNT

Once there was a group of hunters who traveled into dry, rough country to hunt cougar. Now, the splendor of the cougar is well known: it is a tawny, spell-spinning animal whose grace of movement is a match for the legendary desert mountain ranges, ranges full of old stones and fresh mirage.

The three hunters made camp late at night in just such a wilderness range. The campfire burned low, stars wandered through the canyons, sagebrush grew up to the moon. In the morning the three checked their rifles and set out to hunt, separating as they went; each one followed his instincts about the location of the cougar. One of them, a woman, was known as a careful, quick-spirited hunter. She hiked over a saddle and into the thick patches of bitterbrush at the base of a sandstone ridge. The light was spare and clear. She went slowly. She felt strong.

Upon her emergence from the dry luxuriance of the bitterbrush, she found herself near a cliff and face-to-face with a mother cougar and her kittens. The mother, contrary to the stories we hear about cougars, showed neither hostility nor fear; and the woman, contrary to our expectations about hunters, did not raise her rifle. In fact, so forthright, perfect, and full of peace was the confrontation that our hunter by a straightforward and finely conceived operation of heaven felt her hands and feet widened to accommodate fur and pad and the crescent, powerful claws. Her back was inset with muscles so thick that they arched her body down to the ground, and she felt a strange concord with the beauties of the big desert. She felt her new stride, her constellation of teeth, her honey-colored eyes.

Now, to become suddenly a cougar is less moderate a change than many of us undergo in a course of our lives. But our hunter, somehow, understood the purposes it had.

Later during her day as a cougar, after stalking and killing a deer, she was spotted and fired on by one of her own hunting party; the bullet barely grazed her shoulder. That night, when she was a woman again, and had met her friends back at camp, the stories of the cougar that got away gave her as much amusement as the wound in her shoulder gave her pain.

When the trip was over, she returned to her job in the city; but she was not surprised to discover in her life another life, where there was other work to be done—when she was transformed again, and everything around her changed. The streets turned to canyon, dry wash, and rimrock, the windows burst with sage and mesquite; and she hunted to provide food for the kittens.

As she worked at her regular job, the pain in her shoulder always brought to mind what she had learned: that we must hunt day by day, year after year, with hope and care, without giving up, through every merciless change, no matter what the hardships and impossibilities—we must hunt what no one can ever kill.

These phrases and paragraphs are noted down directly from my conversations with a woman in the Basque country of Southern France. She has a marvelous garden, and as she gardened, she talked with me, in her contemplative way. I didn't need to say much of anything. It was as if she were carrying on a conversation with my thoughts.

STATEMENTS SHE PLANTED, THAT GREW UP TO BE STORIES

As independence is to a cat, so are words to a good sentence.

The tree has learned, and with its knowledge has gained the capacity to give sweet fruit. Humans have learned; but often when they gain what their epoch calls *knowledge*, it does not bring any capacity to give love. As a result, knowledge and love are thought to be separate; hence our catastrophes.

So many catastrophes that the trees may stop giving fruit.

The heart is a thundercloud: sometimes lightning, sometimes showers, sometimes a clearing before the winds that blow from a world within this world.

Once it can have its clearing, it can, from then on, call forth any weather necessary.

Paradise is in the dirt anywhere, available once you wink and work in a certain way. Then it comes alive, and it is more than a place, more than reality; rather, the soil of reality, source of forms. This grounding of things, it is thoroughly and roughly alive, has senses of its own. Not earth, it is the way the earth watches us, so that we may be judged. Therefore it is natural to ask, what might be the expression on the face of paradise?

Quizzical. Amorous. Full of longing, rigor, hopefulness, independence. In that expression is the origin of all the come-hither looks given forever.

The military, which has played such a role in our history, is doomed. This is so because, in the long run, only metaphors grow out the barrel of a gun.

....

THE FASHIONABLE LADY AND HER JEWELS

Once upon a time a woman was walking along the streets of her village and stumbled over a big cobblestone that, unlike the many other cobbles she had fallen over, pivoted back like a little door. Revealed within was a shallow cavity jammed with a tattered, oil-stained mass of rags. Now our lady was curious as a young crow, and a scavenger of artful thrift and whimsy. She plucked the unsavory rags from that little den and found that they wrapped an emerald as large as her fist.

She was not easily surprised, and, more than that, not a person to be confused by the inexplicable and magnificent, so she tossed the emerald in a pocket and took it home. And a good thing, too, because she found at home in the mail a little package bearing no return address; and inside the package, a pair of rubies. A fine coincidence! she thought, for now the emerald will have companions.

And she placed them on the table, not meaning, as she turned away, to knock over the sugar bowl.

I'm as clumsy as an animal in its winter fat, she thought; and, cursing and grousing merrily as she reached over to right the bowl, she saw the sugar grains gather and condense into pearls mischievously on the move across the table. And she commenced, in high frenzy and buffoonery, the struggle to keep them from rolling off to the far ends of the earth: around and around she darted, setting up books as a barrier, scooping up pearls, sweeping some toward corners of the room, tossing others toward a big soft chair that soon was studded with the little moons. Carefully, then, she picked up the treasures and placed them in a big mixing bowl with the rubies and emerald. And she thought she was done with these hijinks when she trod upon a neglected pearl. Her feet were whisked from beneath her, and she fell down flat, on the way down knocking over a chair that shattered the glass front of a cabinet full of crockery, demolished a row of glasses, and turned violently on its side a lighted oil lamp.

Maybe I should study ballet, she mused as she lay on her floor after this spectacular demolition of most of her kitchen. And as she got painfully to her feet and stood dimly over the ruins, feeling the bruises bud and flower around her body; as she watched, the flame of the oil lamp, still burning, moved slowly under the power that had threaded together the day's events. It wound from bit to bit of useless glass, from tooth to shard, from sliver to starburst pane, and with the silence we find at flametip transformed every piece of broken glass into a diamond.

This is really getting excessive, she thought; but she knew what to do.

First, with the emerald—she meditated on its vintage clarity; its green like some candent, constant mint spirit; its perfect edge leading her eyes into the midmost of the jewel. And she looked into that place, saw the tranquility there, and after some time of looking she saw the forest, banked and coded within the jewel. All the myriad beauties of the whole forest were present there in her hand, ready to her touch.

She remembered that the local forest had been over the years disappearing under the axe, under the crust of the growing town; and so, day by day, ordinary, ancient, woodland knowledge was being forced from the practical affairs of humankind. To what purpose, then, might a forest be hidden in an emerald?

Our lady decided that she had in her hands a ruse intended to trick humans into recognizing forests as jewels in their own right. The trick would work because emeralds are highly valued due to their rarity, yet forests are infinitely more rare than emeralds; therefore, having been brought to consider the two in association, even humans, logical creatures that they are, should eventually be able to understand that however expensive emeralds may be, a forest is precious beyond reason—precious like justice, peace, stars, and the pleasures of women.

Having concluded all this, she wrapped up the emerald with a note of explanation and sent it off to the local newspaper, which was edited by a woman known as one of the most eloquent people in all the world. Our lady knew that her editor friend would figure out how to publish the story of the gem and its message—and so would the idea held in the emerald be carried far.

She turned from these contemplative labors to her next problem—the pearls. Having figured out the purposes of the emerald, the challenge of the pearls was more tractable. She had long observed that her community (as well as her country—if she could be said to have a country) had seen in recent centuries a melancholy decline in the numbers of visionary men and women active in local affairs. In fact, some thinkers, even many literary critics, had decided that frailty and darkness are dominant in all of us and that imaginative violence is the mark of serious fiction, rather than just a cheap thrill. Pondering the causes of so grotesque an attitude, and their consequence (which is, of course, extinction for us all), she asked herself how she might be of some modest help to her neighborhood using the pearls.

She had noticed, during the walks she took late at night along the dependable river near her home, that the much-beloved iridescence of the waters had lately lost its vigor. There was a tarnishing, a shading, a resignation: and all at once she knew that this very shining— this flourishing of rivers—was the light we needed just now. It is the shining that moves within us, to undo with brightness the habits of mind that fix our gaze upon the mere appearance of things.

So was her course set: the pearls had to be dedicated to the river, if the river, and so our sad eyes, were to have any chance to shine with our normal and destined understanding.

She waited until it was dark. Then, methodically, she gathered up the pearls and carried them out into the

night. She followed the path to the river. In their bur-
lap sack the pearls were clackering. Once by the water,
she flung them, handful after handful, in long arcs like
meteor showers, far out into the current; and she saw
them dissolve in the water as it ran faster. As she turned
away to return home, she left in the middle of the night
the river waters restored, moving like flares from the sun.

Now nothing was left for her labors, save the tough
problems of the rubies and diamonds. Such are the preoccupations of countrywomen. She turned first to the
pair of rubies and saw how elegantly cut they were—not
at all alike—but yet with some poignant shared symmetry, a balance invisible yet indisputable. And beyond
this broad cut of the two stones, she saw that the faces of
the gems were incised with a pattern of their own, a pattern that refined the play of light within and between the
rubies. This play seemed never to be the same; the light
coiled, crossed, vanished: some story was lifted out of
the jewels and given away, some hopefulness held true in
the movement between those two houses of light. And
it occurred to her that, taken together, the two rubies
made a fine metaphor for a couple living together and
loving well: two hearts close but separate, each sharp-
edged with adventures, each marked with a movement
of stories compounded of blood and sunlight; and in the
devotions of day after shared day, giving all they had—
light handed over to life.

She took the rubies down to the center of her little
town, where there was a square used by nearly everyone,
on the way to nearly everywhere. And she placed the
rubies in a hidden place, side by side on a high ledge of the
central fountain where it was customary to sit and talk.

There the rubies could exercise their influence. They are still there, and in the countryside stories tell of that little town, whence so many couples have returned, released into the delectation of a liberty they made together.

Our lady went back home, for she had yet to deal with the diamonds. There were so many! What was to be done? Happily, she thought at once of someone who could decide the proper use of each of these gems, and she gathered them up and wrapped them all together. Then, relaxing, she fixed herself lunch, did some chores; she sang some songs, visited neighbors, told some jokes; and it was already afternoon when she went to town and sent all the diamonds to you.

This woman made her living telling stories to children in Sikkim, in northern India, where there are parti-colored rhododendron forests.

She told me this story almost as soon as she met me, as if I had some life-threatening illness she could see, that she could treat with words.

....

IF SHE ONCE HAD THE GHOST OF A CHANCE AT UNDERSTANDING

It is said that to live well, our understanding must engage the world as we do the work of life; yet to do our work, it has been observed that now and again, we must make ourselves distinct from the world. For the understanding that is immersed always in the passing hours, linked with interminable chains of detail and emotion, joined uncontrollably with the current of everyday concerns, will in the long run lose its life, its clarity, its original powers.

Now, all this once was taught to a woman who, like most of us, had not used her understanding for much of anything in a good long while. She was taught these things, and saved from a terrible fate, by a grocer, a woodworker, and a spider.

To the grocer the woman said: "What is it that makes possible the consumption of so many varied products of the earth?"

The grocer said: "It is because knives and forks are not made of food."

To the woodworker our friend said: "How is it that you are able to shape woods into so many implements useful to humankind?"

The woodworker said: "It is because the tools of a woodworker never have a cutting edge made of wood."

To the spider she said, as though instinctively trying to revive herself: "What rules do you follow in stringing your cobwebs, the center of your life and work?"

The spider said: "I attach my cobwebs to stones, rocks, mountainsides, leaves, telephone poles, anything— but not to other cobwebs."

For many years I made an annual hike in the Grand Canyon, learning my way slowly into that infinite landscape. It is like walking within the heart valves of the continent. Near Thunder River, which pours like a vision from the canyon wall at the base of the Redwall Limestone, I met the woman—also hiking alone—who told me this story about a friend of hers.

....

THE PAINTER OF LIGHT IN THE CANYON OF LIGHT

One day hiking through the twilight deep in the Grand Canyon, near the Colorado River, our friend Lara met the early Renaissance painter Fra Angelico. Her immediate concern, of course, was that she use the proper form of address to greet such a man. Fra? Papa Angelico? My lucid Beato? After all, he had been dead almost eight hundred years, since his splendid and humble painting in Florence, Fiesole, and Rome. All in all, though, she had to admit he looked rather good. He had cast off his friar's robes and was clad in denims and a tattered dark green T-shirt, which showed a rather muscular form.

"Beato," she said, "would you like to share dinner with me?"

"And what will you be having, bambina?" he asked graciously.

"Bourbon, beef jerky, crackers, and cheddar," she said with trepidation.

"I'd be delighted," he said with the savor of a man confirmed in elemental pleasures.

And as they settled at the bend of the river in a sandy cove, Fra Angelico told her of his new work.

"You will remember my labors trying to bring together heaven and earth using only oil paints and dry wood; and then, later, the hope and sorrows of the frescos of San Marco," he said. "I was a messenger of innocent, mindful forms; figures that move by operation of will become an internal circulation of light."

"So many now have seen them," she said.

"To have seen them is nothing," he replied softly. "But to have made use of them, to commence a traveling within life—such is the invitation of those paintings. May you go to the place I was myself taken."

The Fra leaned back against a beautifully worn limestone slope. Listening to him, Lara could not help but think that there is much to be gained in the company of the voluble, satisfied dead. In fact, it seemed evident that conversation, if it might have a perfect, rough forthrightness, held its place in a pattern of ideas and events that extended into the next world.

"And so what are you doing here?" Lara asked brusquely.

He looked at her with patient bemusement.

"I *am* here," he said. "Or more precisely, I am here and there."

"No," Lara said impatiently, "what are you *doing* here?"

"I am being this place," he said with aplomb.

They paused in their conversation while Lara mulled this one over. The time passed easily enough in the raw simplicity of the canyon. After her ruminations it was still twilight, and Fra Angelico was still there, looking askance at her.

"You understand nothing," he observed cheerfully.

"My conclusion exactly," she admitted.

"In just this part of the canyon, just these days, I am the canyon," he went on, eating crackers and looking around carelessly. "I was given this job at death, since that is the time when the soul, which during physical life retains its little human preferences, can have the chance, if it is prepared, to take on another form, one apposite to its future labors. Now, you know that in my painting I was the devotee, the aficionado, the flourisher of light; and so did the power that comes to instruct our wandering souls come for me, and grant me a chance to continue my studies here in the canyon. And why here? Well, just look around, young woman! This canyon is one of the few on earth that can serve as a proving ground, a school, a playing field, a pleasance of light. It's the only place big enough.

"I live here, work here. I may take on the consistency of stone, that lifts up its head in the weather, to be broken and land in the flashing river and somersault in the currents year after year. I can inhabit a butte, a side canyon, a promontory, rimrock and sheer ledge, or the wall of flowers just beyond a beautiful spring of clear water. And always I am watching the light in all weathers, I am bearing the light and being its student, reflecting, passing on the radiance, working to understand that bright movement which brings this place to the eyes of you who visit here.

"I can, as I choose, recompose myself as a man, so as to appear to the occasional strange one like you. Also, I like a glass of Barolo now and then. But otherwise I have been here working for eight hundred years."

"Eight hundred years!"

"I have lots of time," he explained patiently.

"And so . . ." Lara asked.

"Soon I will move on to my next task," he said. "I'd hate to see all this labor go to waste."

"What on earth can you do next?"

"Once I have learned all the silken tricks of light, the foregathering and breakings-through, the deliverance and subtle propositions, the scattering and fantastication of color—once the work is done, and I am qualified, I will myself become light."

"For heaven's sake! No one can become light," Lara said with authority.

But then she looked around, and it was dark.

This story from Acushla is about her youth. She was at the time trying to find the best way for the mind to come into concord with the movement of desire. Or for desire to make its peace with a more permanent and instructive beauty. She has a pacific, capacious soul and an amorous disposition. She lives presently on a farm in Vermont.

....

THE SWEETNESS OF LIFE GIVES A GAL ODD HABITS

Even as a teenage girl, Acushla had concluded that life was sweet; unfortunately, this conviction estranged her from most of her would-be friends, whose hearts careened through the world in a tempest of anxiety. Anxiety was a fascinating thing to Acushla—very unpredictable, a colossus of the psyche—that went brusquely through brain and bones, through intentions, hopes, preferences, decisions, ideas, sweeping all aside in favor of its own preoccupations.

Acushla, however, thought that it was all a good deal simpler than it looked. In fact, she decided, based on her study of herself and everyone she knew, that anxiety in the human creature had two themes, and two only:

1) I might not get what I want, or
2) I might get what I want, and *then* what will I do?

As if this were not enough, Acushla noted that these desires often involved other people, who, of course, had their own agendas and anxieties; and so the whole show was made more complex and dangerous than ever.

Our heroine adopted a simple, rustic technique: labor. She replaced desire with effort, and to hell with the consequences. Instead of wanting bread, for instance, she concentrated on the grain, the salt, the yeast, the butter, the technique, and the labor of baking. If bread resulted, she ate it; if not, she stayed in the school of study and of hunger.

Instead of wanting a lover, she studied the arts of love, she readied herself for the iridescence of pleasure, she tried to envision a life where word and touch, hope and idea, were made into a gift for someone else, each day, as she lived. And when lovers came into her brilliant days and moved with her through the hot, confident nights, she lived with them, so long as they stayed, in the midmost of the world reserved for lovers who are thoughtful and thankful.

In other words, Acushla had excised from her life, as one would a tumor, the notion of reward; instead, she gave herself to learning, to readiness; and when a gift came her way, she recognized it.

Of course, everyone thought she was arrogant because she seemed to know what she was doing, because she was at no one's mercy, and because she did not bemoan her fate. Some, naturally, even saw her as an uncompromising, distant woman. What they resented is that they could neither control her nor define her.

She could make stolid friends funny. She could bring to an ignominious phrase an apt metaphor, could disrupt with exultation the august conclusions of men. She could banish the stink of melancholy with the spices of her jokes, her teasing, her hijinx, her shenanigans.

Acushla, as time went on, as a result of her offbeat initiatives, learned from all the world, and the life in the world. She was able to conceal her abilities within, and so few people knew how she strode through the world with the stealth of a jaguar, she scudded like a cloud, she shone like a crescent moon: that is, only those lucky enough to love her understood her rich, wild mind.

As she portrayed herself, she was just another run-of-the-mill female living out her life. Just another neighbor.

Such is her simple story. Now, she admitted that there were many who claimed that work is done only in desire of reward. This, she noted, is the same as thinking that life leads only to death.

However, if life may lead to life, and (as an additional bonus) death may do the same, it is logically necessary that she continue to live by what she saw as our soul's first and best joke. Namely, that the only desire that has any reality is to find out what is worth desiring. We need to know. What if, for example, it turns out that we cannot really learn how to want anything until we already have it?

Heard in the town of Independence, California, from a woman who knows and cherishes Death Valley. She has hiked its somber and hallucinatory canyons for ten years.

....

A WOMAN COMING FOR LOVE

Our friend Clarissa, so beautiful that in her town the sun rose through her room, was thinking one day about the earth sciences, as they relate to our survival; and she came easily to the conclusion that stones have spirits. After all, if you lived for thousands of years, and held in your substance old stories about millenniums of events on earth; if you had found a durable form and a splendid tranquility, how might you want to manifest yourself on earth? What are your real choices?

Certainly you would not choose the human form— there is no room anymore for such helpful and durable people on earth. In any case, you then would have to go through, more than once, the whole elaborate and theatrical business of pretending to die. And more difficult yet: even if such a woman survived the uncontrollable hatred loosed upon anyone who suggests that a permanent life is worth having, and who has a method for making such a life, she would still be subject to the flattery and curiosity of those who wanted something from her. And as everyone knows, the admiration of people is as dangerous as their hatred.

And so it was that Clarissa went to the desert, into a canyon full of stones, so full that just to walk in the big streambed of the canyon set up a maniacal clattering, a bounding and ricocheting all along the rock walls: she felt as if she were participating in an avalanche. But she walked onward, for she was sure that she would find herself in the full company of voluble, informative tricksters.

Once far enough into the canyon, she sat down on a ledge and surveyed her companions. So did they survey her. She noted immediately that the sounds of her moving up the canyon had been her introduction to the language of stones—a statement of basic phonetics and grammar. But phonetics and grammar, while they have their uses, do not address the real problems of learning a language. It is semantics, the science of meaning, that demands seasoning, lightheartedness, exultations, and steadfast peace—only by possessing such qualities might a woman learn.

And so it was that our young beauty, who would otherwise have been wielding a jackhammer, a welding torch, a scalpel, or an optical spectrometer, came instead to be deep in a canyon trying to talk to stones.

Eventually she succeeded. She discovered the ordinary thing: that the land itself sets forth in plain language a whole wild set of useful notions. Using only essential elements, it can teach about essentials only. Instead of using words to convey a meaning, the language of earth must use its most widely available material—that is, it must use rock. In other words, the pursuits of metaphysics, aesthetics, religion: they may be replaced, for some students, by one intensive course in geology. This would simplify many an academic program.

To cite only a very few examples, among the many Clarissa came to know in her excursions: a walker in open country may come upon a butte that will teach her how to stand fast and calm in a storm of events. The slow windings of a summer canyon may teach, by their patience and sinuosity, the manner of movement in an afternoon's lovemaking (preeminent among metaphysical excursions) that leads its lovers to unknown regions in the province of pleasure. The mountain valley built with grace around the clear stream may teach a woman how to gather her days around the current that runs inside life, how to keep that current at the center of her years, how to learn beauty from the movement of beauty.

Now, it will certainly be objected that since land and humans are so different, the qualities possessed by rock in all its richness and propositions would be of little use to us. Those who have such objections have no chance of winning to heart and bed the beautiful Clarissa, who, amorous, philosophical, tough as stone, soft as dust, even now is walking from the canyons— into a story, toward you.

Told to me in Venice, near the Arsenale. The teller was a history student who claimed she had gathered these facts from the secret letters of the lover of an enigmatic medieval king.

....

SHE WRITES ABOUT THE KING SHE LOVES

Once upon a time there was a man who wanted to be king; and because of his hard work and whole heart, by the rigor of his mind and the beauty of his sentences, he was indeed proclaimed king. Now, it was customary in his country that coronations be celebrated by a grand effort of engineering and architecture; and this time it was decided that a magnificent bridge be constructed. The bridge was to be completed on coronation day, and opened so that his majesty, newly crowned, could walk with his celebrating and beloved people onto a great suspended road of bold pier, filigreed iron, and flaring cable.

However, when the great moment came, it was discovered the bridge lacked a small but indispensable supporting strut, and so was unsafe to tread upon. Desperately, the builders cast about for some metal they could twist and weld into place, so that the ceremony could go on. But they reported unhappily that a suitable piece could not be found.

At that moment, the king stepped forward:

"The solution is simple," he said. "Ready your hammers and welding fires—and take my crown."

"Your majesty," replied the builders, "you must keep your crown. You are a king, and this is coronation day."

"All this is so," he said, "but what is the job of a king? It is to support his subjects on their way; so take my crown, that this bridge may bear them securely. On this first day of my reign, may I not be so unworthy as to let pass this chance to do for my people the service of a man who would be king."

And thus it was that the work was finished, the music commenced, the bridge opened to the great crowds. So great was the press of citizens that the uncrowned king was lost to view. No one had any doubt, however, that he was there among his people. Later that day, of course, I knew exactly where he was: in my bed.

Everyone has taken up the work of the court. The country is productive, peaceful, beautiful, yet full of wild initiatives. It is so because of its people: though they are happy, they have learned that there is no end to thankfulness, that peace holds riches that show the gains of vainglory to be absurd, and that love and learning are two words that refer to the same resurgent life within. That is, the people of our country are distinguished not by the magnificence of a single throne, but by a royalty of so many hearts.

At last, the triumph of monarchy: a king can learn to be a man. And then, as a man, if he is lucky, he has the chance to learn to be a husband.

Then he can learn anything.

By the side of Mono Lake sits the small town of Lee Vining, California. In the wonderful bookstore there, I met a woman fascinated by the Transfiguration, because of the many parallel accounts of such changes in the lives of those who, privately, have perfected themselves. She observed that transfiguration, apparently, does not need to take place on a mountaintop; yet it seems always to be a phenomenon of light.

She went on to tell me this story of her illness and recovery.

....

A VISITATION OF COMETS

Everyone will be familiar with the motes of dust in the air, visible when light slants through a room. But it turns out that not all such specks of dust have the same origin, nor the same purpose. There are always those who think that dust has no purpose. And they are right, when it is only dust. There are those who think the heart has no purpose. They are right, when it is only a pump. But I must say, even at the risk of being despised, that if both dust and hearts have other uses, then every room, every house, the earth itself, is changed forever, as if by a slow but incendiary transfiguration.

I will tell you how I know this. I live in the south-western part of North America, a place where rock sounds with the clangor of sunlight. I once was sick, very sick, and I heard of a woman who lived far out across a mesa, who was said to be made of light. I dragged myself in her direction, and later, on the way, a kind man folded me over his donkey and led me along dusty roads. He left me with a boatman who took me across a cobalt river to the mouth of a canyon. He rowed the boat up on the sand and carried me up the canyon to a stone house alongside a stream. The house was almost invisible.

In fact, the woman who lived there was almost invisible. I didn't even see her, even though she was standing a few feet away from me. Then, when the light was low and slanted through the canyon, I saw a sparkling that looked to have a human form. And I heard her voice.

"Come with me, onto my porch, and we will sit together. I am the keeper of this canyon; and for this one night I am your keeper, as well."

And all at once I could see her, in the flesh. She was a slight, plain woman, with a look on her face of sharp loving and raucous curiosity. She led me to the porch. We sat and talked in the twilight, listening to the stanzas of the stream, watching the juniper and pinyon pine gather the soft darkness. She did nothing but tell me stories, and so effortlessly that her voice moved like a companion to the passage of the stream over stone.

Later, she took me inside and helped me into a bed, and she sat by my side for a long time. She touched my face lightly and whispered to me. Through the window I saw the moon rise, mindful and curious, over the canyon wall.

In the morning I felt so well, I could hardly recognize myself. And I felt bold enough to ask some questions.

Over breakfast (it was buckwheat biscuits), I said:

"How is it that you sometimes are so hard to see?"

"It's a simple thing," she replied. "It has to do with comets."

"Comets?" I asked skeptically. Though I must admit that being in that house gave me the odd feeling of moving through space.

"Every day the earth is hit by small comets. They break up in the atmosphere, and nothing more is seen of them. Yet when they break up, their motes of dust drift to earth. They are almost invisible, except in the light. But light is a substance—everyone has known, since Einstein, that light has mass. So it is that these infinitesimal motes of dust, after their journey through space, come here newly composed. That is, they are composed principally of light, as they descend to earth.

"As they descend, they do so watchfully, these celestial messengers.

"Have you ever seen iron filings, the minute threads, collect around a magnet? In just the same way, these motes of light collect around anyone whose own internal lights are beginning to shine. They gather around such a person, they saturate her; until finally they recreate her. One day she, too, is composed of moving lights, a bounty and mystery of moving lights.

"So it was with me. It means many things; it means, for instance, that I can heal."

I could see that our conversation was ending because she was becoming more translucent.

"I cannot stay healthy until I know what you know," I said quickly.

"Then abandon this nonsense of living from dust to dust, with an interval of faith. From the sickness of faith, see your way to the healing offered everywhere, every day, in the very air. You will know, as you look and live, that the dust of what we are is meant to make a material of light. The world is a place, and a summons. My beloved friend, consider the patience of the earth, as it waits for us—"

"How do I . . ." I began to ask.

But there was nothing left of her but sparkling, and the downcanyon breeze took her off through rock walls, along the streambed, toward the big blue river.

Or, as some would have it: the random wind blew the useless dirt down the canyon, where it will be scattered by chance across ground and water, to choke us, or stain us. Later, to bury us.

A story from a woman who lived along the Truckee River, in Northern Nevada. This river links two lakes sacred to the Indian peoples of this region, Lake Tahoe and Pyramid Lake. These lakes, and the river, are said to hold secrets, to promote healing, and to offer urgently an uncommon way into the world.

....

A LUMINOUS NEWSPAPER

It was autumn and a woman was walking along a river. She loved this time—the beginning of twilight, when after hours of bright-eyed wandering through the day, the light began to take into its arms the darkness. And soon she came upon a small park and found at its very edge a newspaper stand. It was the ordinary sort of stand, of painted metal cold and hard as the usual news, yet the paper inside was placed so that the headlines were invisible—all she could tell was that those headlines were not of familiar typeface and layout, and so probably the publication was not that of any of the regional newspaper companies. What was more, the stand itself had no slots to take coins, and the paint was of a peculiar watery color that made it almost invisible against the river. In fact (the woman realized with a start) the stand faced the river, away from the sidewalk where strollers might likely see it. She wondered who was meant to buy these papers. The fishes, maybe?

Our friend had discovered the stand only as a consequence of her walking as close to the water as she could. She did this because the reflections thrown forth by the river held for her extravagant fascination and continuous promise. And now, as she could not resist her attraction to the eccentric newspaper stand, she decided to obtain a newspaper from it, if such purchase was possible. First, she tugged at the stand; it did not open. Then she noticed the instructions, almost illegible from the effects of rain, heat, and river mist. They read: PRICE: ONE CARTWHEEL.

Now, our friend was no expert in cartwheels—just walking about, she thought, was spectacle enough—but a rambunctious curiosity kept her from departing. And so, after some deliberation and a little prayer that she be kept from permanent injury, she laughed her way through a passable cartwheel; and as she regained her feet, the latch on the stand popped open.

Eagerly she took up the newspaper. It was thick. The headline read: THREE CROWS TO SPEAK AT DAWN TOMORROW. As if this pronouncement were not strange enough, the columns of news were arranged in a kind of impeccable confusion: some of the columns proceeded from the bottom of the page to the top; some were read from the right margin to the left, and some the reverse; and some columns even started at the top of the page, just as in an ordinary newspaper. In order to read the front page, our friend had to turn the paper in all directions, as though it were a little planet revolving in her hands.

The content of the newspaper was amused, generous, and arcane. At column end of some of the front-page stories, she found instructions like this: "Story discontinued," or "See Page 45, which this paper may or may not have, according to the chances of history." Sometimes when a reference to an inner page was present, the continued story would start with a sentence like "The story on the front page was a fraudulent lie; having got this far, Dear Reader, you deserve the truth," or "For the remainder of this story, please phone so and so," or "The reporter confesses being stupefied by this story and begs the reader to supply an inventive conclusion."

Yet others of the articles in the paper seemed to introduce stories already finished, or, alternatively, to be finished by events set in motion by the newspaper itself. One might find the notice "Story continued on Page 14 of the edition of this newspaper issued exactly one hundred thirty-three years ago," or "The following events have not yet occurred, but they will," or even "The following article describes something that should have happened yesterday or the day before." One article was headlined NEWSPAPER LOSES ITS TEMPER and related how, when one of its readers was sensed to have been reading in too self-possessed and grave a manner, the newspaper had, in a fit of passion, torn itself to pieces.

But most noteworthy of all in the newspaper was the subject of some of the pieces. There were the usual descriptions, in however prophetic and mischievous a manner, of the affairs of state and the deeds of humankind; but the greater part of the stories concerned a world that resembled this one, or perhaps a world that daily life is meant to resemble.

Our friend read through the main article of the day, concerning the crows. It explained the expected arrival at dawn of three crows who had spent their lives flying up all the rivers of the world, in order to compare their headwaters, so that they might form some conclusions about the sources of beauty. After completion of that task, they had gone to the songbirds to teach them all they had learned, and to ask them to sing their learning, since crows, as we know, cannot themselves sing. And so at dawn, the crows were going to meet together and introduce their travels in plain language, and then appeal to us, that if we would understand our rivers, we must listen: and by the songs of birds we will be taught the origin and grace of these moving waters.

Feeling better informed already, our friend moved on to another story which examined the important questions of human destiny and, by use of etymology, psychology, veterinary medicine, economics, mycology, puns, and arithmetic, proved that for some portion of humankind it really would be possible not to be killed off by melancholy. Yet another article described the discovery that the street layouts of every landlocked city on earth bore an exact and predictable relation to the layout of nerve cells in the brain of the common dolphin.

All these stories so spellbound our friend that, even though no one can read in the dark, she sat in darkness reading them; and she had just finished the back page, a transcript of an interview with a group of fireflies, when she saw it was dawn.

She noticed that another edition of the paper had been placed in the newsstand, and, by executing an accomplished cartwheel, she got a copy. The headline was NEWSPAPER WINS NEW READER, and she read a long story about herself that included certain future events, like for example the day, hour, and delicious situation when a man she knew would fall in love with her. And so was she privileged for months with an old-fashioned simmering anticipation, and was better able to prepare her heart and life, so that she might be able to judge well what journeying in the countries of love she should do with that gentleman.

It will be noticed, in all this, that our newspaper had no title. Instead, it had headlines, stories, articles, interviews. All we can say is that it is the oldest newspaper in the world, that its writers never cease their labors, that its stands are everywhere, and that it is published every day, at sunrise.

When I am traveling, I have the custom of asking the stranger next to me on the bus, the train, the airplane; on the trail, or in the café—of asking the old-fashioned questions; that is, about the weather, contemporary politics, the relation of language to reality, the nature of the soul, and other mundane topics. A woman on the overnight train from Paris to Madrid almost spat out this answer. It's all she said. I translate, as in some other stories here, from Spanish.

I never saw her again.

....

SOUL, WORDS, GOD:
SHE'S GOT ISSUES

People say nowadays, in our advanced and glittering epoch, that the body has no soul. If it's there, they say, why cannot we see it, touch it, find it once and for all? That may be so, we say, but take the meaning of words— can you see it, touch it, find it once and for all?

They reply predictably: words have no meaning.

We ask: What do you mean by that? But they don't laugh.

Neither do they laugh when we go on to discuss the location of the soul. The reasoning goes like this: if the soul (as has been established by researchers in the field) is that part of the body which may be made permanent by love, then, for those who have found a way to the midmost of life, by such adventures, for just such common folk, while their bodies are alive, the body *is* the soul.

Now the sophisticates *can* touch it. And they're still not satisfied.

THERE SEEMS TO be a debate about whether or not God plays with dice—as if these were the only two choices. But according to graffiti found on walls in little bars in wild country in western North America, a different conception might be useful. God works like this: she sometimes rolls the dice; she sometimes sets the rules and gives us the dice, and the rules change according to who is playing, and their company. Or to put it another way, because we live in a universe refined by chance, we have a chance. Or to put it another way, sometimes she is the dice; sometimes she travels as thunderbolt and insect; she changes gender; he plays lead guitar and gives speeches late at night to boisterous and happy friends; he loves you, and you can tell, because the curve of his arm as he embraces you matches the arc of the crescent moon.

She does none of these things, all of these things. But when she acts, what he does resembles these things. What does not change is what he means by this moving inside the worlds.

She means peace.

THE WORLD IS getting to be superlatively skilled in telling things apart. Anyone can tell you how one thing differs from another, how to make this distinction or that.

There are definitions, degrees, categories, glossaries, lists, hierarchies. And all these things codify by much useful work the marking off of one thing from another.

But what of the resemblances of things? Where is the language that, in the finest gradations, sets out the labor, the tricks, the forthright beauty and authority of likeness?

How does heaven resemble earth? What does the passage of starlight have to do with the movement of desire? Does the curl of a flower petal in the morning match the unfolding of an idea in the imagination of a child? Is the silence in a big dry canyon like the silence in the eye of a hurricane in mid-ocean?

When the light falls on the body of the woman you love, and her skin shines with sweat, why is the whole world illumined by that shining, why is that world the homeland you recognize at last?

THE LOCATION OF the soul, the character of god, the current of resemblance that unifies this world and all others: these are three subjects. Think of them as a band in a bar: a lead guitar, a bass, drums. They need a fourth, a singer.

Step right up.

A story about a carpenter, told by a carpenter. She lives on the coast of Maine, and she built the most beautiful sailboat I have ever seen. After she told me this story, I wondered about the uses of its beauty. And to what destinations she might sail.

....

THE CARPENTER OF THE HEART

Once upon a time there was a woman who was carpenter of the heart. She could, by means of her constructions in rare woods, change the very cardiac inclinations of those who saw her work. For instance, by inlaying rosewood, ebony, and birch in a subtle pattern, a tabletop she created could cause certain people to remember all their dreams, and to know how the threads of those dreams are meant to be spun into the tapestry of daily affairs.

Another time, she designed a chair that made humans honest: everyone who sat in this chair and talked could not stop themselves from telling the truth. She made, as well, a little house no bigger than a breadbox that elves could not resist. All someone had to do was to take this little house and put it in a bedroom, and soon enough they would be able to talk privately to the elves who would make it their permanent residence. Now elves, of course, are ancient and enduring projects of the earth and carry a high energy of heart; like most of the important things in our lives, they are generally thought to be unreal. But even so, they give all sorts of outrageous, mantic, useful advice about a life that is within this life.

Now it was necessary for our carpenter friend to keep secret what she had discovered about the possibilities within carpentry, for her strange, happy work was not understood by every friend and neighbor. So most people thought she was an ordinary carpenter, and that her hands held not the saga of her blood and her humor and our future. When she died, almost no one mourned her.

The pieces of work, of course, remain. Here and there you may find a tabletop of ingenious, unnerving inlay, a chair of uncanny, graceful lines, or an extraordinary little house. It was the hope of the carpenter that these and other pieces of hers would be found, and that people would eventually use them to explore her methods, and apply them to their chosen, daily, ordinary labors—so that one day we might see mechanics hard at work in a repair shop for every model of the heart, mathematicians proving theorems with uncanny axioms offered by the heart, farmers tending rich soil found only in the garden of the heart. Now, we may ask, what would such people really do?

It's difficult to say. What do you do?

These paragraphs were written out for me by a novelist in London. She is the only writer I know to publish under three different pen names; for each name, she has a different writing style and preferred genre. She is famous under two of those names. She has concealed successfully her identity for over three decades.

....

WHAT SHE TOLD ME ABOUT WHY SHE WRITES

The writer's task is just a fantastical way to get set for annihilation in the dark of sod. Luckily, this can be done by just going along, barreling along, galumphing into the future with no more knowledge than a rutabaga of what might happen to you.

So it's a good thing rutabagas can be grown in gardens, because it demonstrates what, with care and cultivation, might still be possible for us.

Whatever happens, one thing is certain: We will be called on to remember what we were, how we grew, whether we made the least effort to produce anything that counts. And what tender shoots we put forward into the next world. And whether we were visited with a blessing: after long labors, to look in the mirror and see nothing, nothing at all. If we were so lucky, in that mirror we could see a world full of strangers, and know once again our longing for their fortune, their thriving, the presence in them of powerful beauties. We have our one chance and our one life to love them with language. And we have our chance to do so, because work in language, with time, is anonymous.

THERE IS NOTHING more homely than writing—it is an old-fashioned preparation for, as Rumi said, annihilation in the light of God. Luckily, this can be done as a natural part of the day, as sentences form within you in any corner grocery store, in an old car puttering down the highway, or while shoveling horse manure, tending bar, or just shuffling around the streets, mulling things over.

To put it another way: if you want to write in hopes that your phrases might be tasty to the mind and useful to the spirit of your reader, then you better be ready to go out and get some down-and-dirty, honky-tonk, wide-ranging, classical education: you have to write after dipping your pen in spice pods filled with clear distillations of wild good books, filled with rainwater, whiskey, salty residue of tide pools, sacramental wine, olive oil, sweat, pond water in wilderness canyons, the elixir of life. With such ink, your language will be plain, clear, direct.

TO TAKE ANOTHER approach entirely: write so that in this world, a couple in love will want to cook with your work, find some place for you, some minute nourishment in what you have done; to use you as one ingredient in a dish that they are making for one other, as a gift to one another, given freely, given without expectation.

Whatever they cook, it is their lives they taste. What they taste comes from the kitchen, from what they think, what they read, how they praise, the way they give thanks. So is work in language a prayer: and it may be that from the shelf, every now and then, you have been one of the hundreds of items taken down, and that, in the smallest way, briefly, occasionally, when it makes sense in the recipe, you can be of use to them, serve them, please them, make them smile, be present only in your vanishing. But still you can hope for them, love them.

What matters, of course, is that the meal is forgotten, and that the two lovers go—easy, fragrant, teasing, mellifluous—off to bed.

What matters is that only they matter—the two of them, the spark in the one, the kindling of heaven in the other.

Heard in bed, in a cabin in the rain forest on the island of Dominica, of the Lesser Antilles, in the Caribbean. For some, the arts of love include the arts of pillow talk.

The island has more extensive cover of rain forest than any of the other islands in the region, and it has brightly colored, phosphorescent pools that border a boiling lake.

....

IN THE HOT CLIMATE OF PROMISES AND GRACE

A woman's languor in bed in the morning by the sea in the tropics—what beauty does not belong to her?

On the island, far in the forests, currents of rainwater burst over ledges to fall into big cool deep green pools.

She knows this.

She laughs to think how generally it is conceived that lovemaking is an instinctual, private indulgence; a full bolt of merely physical rapture. In fact, such pleasures are of so entirely distinct an order that they should have another name entirely, to mark them out more vividly—a name to clarify the way, by such embraces, life may be recomposed. Or a name that we must invent, even as we reinvent ourselves, as a natural part of our coming home to a commonwealth we make together.

They are themselves, these moments, more than us. They are, she thinks, a trustworthy wildfire of detail, reverence, adoration—of reunion and remembrance. They hold our chance to learn how to tease each other at last out of our lives. They are the way for us to witness in an hour the story of years—how we might fuse lights held within so that flesh is lost unexpectedly, in fateful visitation—our vanishing together.

Lovers' antics—a theatre for two in which each helps the other practice the joinery of body and soul— our one undressed rehearsal. A clown-show with all-spice and silence. A simple question with a thousand and one improvised and classical answers. A ragtag, roughed-up, nitty-gritty music. Mischief, experiment, a future, our peace—

Her lover turns to her, comes close, smiles at her. He asks her what, in her languor, she has been thinking.

She tells him everything, and then says: "I've figured out why love is never named as one of the sacraments: it's because it includes all the others."

AFTERWORD

There comes a time when, after many travels, a man needs to be at home. This is especially so if that home is somewhere he might, as it were, travel in place.

In such travels, I remember every day the women whose friendship and mischief have made me the man I am: that is, the women in this book. My good fortune is to have listened to many more of their stories; you have here a rather small selection. Yet I trust that now you have a sense of the work—and the play—of these women.

Why did clay turn to an opal in that woman's hand?

A movement of dragonflies in the afternoon sunlight of a river canyon: are they writing in air the names of the myriad stars in the minds of children?

Is that a pinwheel galaxy in the garden?

If I might state the obvious: I have provided these stories not just so that you know about these women. I wanted them to know about you. This introduction having been made, I leave you in one another's company.

NOTES

PART I

PHOTO

An image, from 1857, of a woman who may well be Emily Dickinson, the greatest poet in American history, and one of the greatest in world history, with an unparalleled range of subject, a powerful and legendary diction, and a bold, radiant form. The image was discovered in the Amherst College Special Collections and has been the subject of intense scholarly debate and study.

QUOTES

Neruda: #14 from *20 poemas de amor y una canción deses-perada,* in his *Obras Completas,* 1957, published by Losada.

On Dickinson: the complete works of Emily Dickinson now exist in two separate editions, the first edited by Thomas H. Johnson, published in 1951, and a more recent edition, in 1998, edited by R. W. Franklin. Dickinson's poems have different numbers in each edition. This quote is from poem #1069 in the Johnson edition, and

#1125 in the Franklin edition. Both editions are published by Harvard University Press.

The quote from Kafka is aphorism #14 in the series of numbered aphorisms, each of them on separate sheets of paper, and found among the writer's papers. I read it in the Shocken edition, 1970, in the book *The Great Wall of China: Stories and Reflections*.

Frank Cushing was an American anthropologist who traveled to New Mexico with John Wesley Powell in the late 1800s, and decided to stay with the Zuni. He lived in their pueblo from 1879 to 1884 and received the name "Medicine Flower." The quote is from his book *Zuni Fetiches*, written in 1883, and published by the Smithsonian Institution.

PART II

Photo
Émilie du Châtelet, born in 1706, was the daughter of a courtier of Louis XIV and was educated in languages, science, and mathematics. She was the translator of Isaac Newton's *Principia Mathematica* into French and was a formidable physicist in her own right, even correcting some of Newton's errors. She had a husband, and many lovers, among whom was Voltaire. The pair lived together for a number of productive years at her chateau in Lorraine.

Quotes
Yu Xuanji was a courtesan and Taoist teacher in China in the 9th C. This verse is taken from the book *Women*

in Praise of the Sacred, 1994, edited by the poet Jane Hirshfield and published by HarperCollins.

Li Qingzhao was a poet and artist in China in the early 12th C. Her work is now celebrated wherever poetry is read and studied. This quote is also from *Women in Praise of the Sacred*.

Emily Dickinson's letter to her sister is from 1864, during a spell of years in which Dickinson wrote in what can only be called a torrent of genius. It is in her *Selected Letters*, 1958, Harvard University Press.

Rabia el-Adawia was a Sufi saint of the 8th C. This quote is from the 2015 edition of *The Way of the Sufi*, by Idries Shah, published by the Idries Shah Foundation in London.

PART III

PHOTO

Mary Wollstonecraft, born in 1759, began an independent life at the age of nineteen after suffering for years in a household ruled by an abusive, irresponsible father. She was a writer, translator, and original thinker, and in 1792 published her *Vindication of the Rights of Woman*, an extraordinary, decisive advance in thinking about woman's rights and human rights. She had two children out of wedlock and married both of the men who had fathered her children.

QUOTES

Nobuko Katsura was a modern Japanese poet and a specialist in haiku. She died in 2004. This poem is taken
from the book *Love Haiku*, 2015, translated and edited
by Patricia Donegan with Yoshie Ishibashi, and published by Shambhala.

The verse from ancient Sumer is probably by Kubatum,
a priestess. The lines, according to Jane Hirshfield in
Women in Praise of the Sacred, celebrate the devotions of
Kubatum's marriage to the king, in a sacred rite recalling
the marriage of Inanna and Damuzi.

Hakim Sanai was a Sufi poet who lived in Afghanistan in
the 12th C. The line is from his book *The Walled Garden
of Truth*, 1974, Octagon Press, translated by David
Pendlebury.

"Thunder: Perfect Mind" is a long poem found in the
Nag Hammadi Library, 1988. The poem is translated
by George W. MacRae, in the revised edition of these
Gnostic scriptures edited by James M. Robinson, and
published by Harper and Row.

PART IV

PHOTO

Sor Juana Inés de la Cruz was born around 1651 in
Mexico. She grew into a beautiful young woman of
lustrous intelligence and turned down many marriage
proposals in order to devote herself to a life of study. In
1667, she began her life as a nun, assembled thereafter

a considerable personal library, and studied both theology and the poets of the Golden Age in Spain. She was a poet, scholar, dramatist, and passionate defender of the right of women to seek knowledge, write verse, and practice philosophy. She is celebrated as the first published feminist in the New World.

QUOTES

Ikuyo Yoshimura is a prize-winning contemporary Japanese poet, a professor of English, and head of the Evergreen circle, a group whose writers compose haiku in English. This quote is from *Love Haiku*.

Shakespeare's line is from Act 1, scene i, of *Measure for Measure*.

Nawab Jan-Fishan Khan was a warrior and Sufi sage who lived in the 19th C. This quote is taken from *The Way of the Sufi*, by Idries Shah, the 20th-C Sufi scholar who is a descendent of Jan-Fishan Khan.

The Dickinson quatrain is #1235 in the Johnson edition and #1245 in the Franklin edition.

ACKNOWLEDGMENTS

A book of stories by and about women must naturally owe the most to the two extraordinary women I live with: my loving and resourceful wife, Lucy Blake, who is steadfast in her defense of the beauties of the earth; and my daughter, Gabriella, of lustrous and independent mind—she has been her whole life my teacher.

This book and my previous one, *Granada: A Pomegranate in the Hand of God*, are both published by Counterpoint Press, which is a most admirable enterprise, full of professionals who do mindful, daily, careful work. The editorial director of Counterpoint is Jack Shoemaker, in whose debt I stand: he is a prodigiously gifted editor, and a patient, deeply learned man. Any writer in the country would be lucky to work with him.

A special thanks to Saira Shah and Tahir Shah. Both of them have done work of such courage and value. That they think these stories worthy of their time and support means the world to me.

The writer and musician Robert Leonard Reid read an early draft of these stories and kindly encouraged me in my labors. The magisterial Joe Crowley also read them, and his good opinion cheered me considerably. Christine Kelly, owner of the Sundance Bookstore in Reno, Nevada, keeps literary culture alive in the West, and I am but one writer who looks upon her with love and respect. One night by the fireplace in a ranch house in the Sierra Nevada my friends Richard Nevle, Deborah Levoy, and Sophie Nevle Levoy generously listened to some of these stories, and helped me to think through the madly complex issue of the title for so exotic a volume.

Elizabeth Dilly, *la maravillosa*, worked with me at every stage and with every detail of this book. It would not exist without her, and so is it justly dedicated to her.